The Beethoven Sequence

THE BEETHOVEN SEQUENCE

by Gerald Elias

LEVEL
BEST BOOKS

ISBN: 978-1-947915-87-9 (hardcover)

First edition

ISBN: 978-1-947915-84-8

Cover art by Level Best Designs

This book was professionally typeset on Reedsy.
Find out more at reedsy.com

Dedicated to my children, Kate and Jacob, who keep me on my toes.

Plaudite, amici, comedia finite est.

Applaud, my friends, the comedy is over.

LUDWIG VAN BEETHOVEN, ON HIS DEATHBED.
MARCH, 1827

Contents

II   UTOPIA RAZED

Praise for Books by Gerald Elias

"The twists and turns of his plotting will leave the reader guessing."—*Booklist* for *Danse Macabre*

"There's just one word for this book: bravo!"—*Publishers Weekly* for *Death and Transfiguration*

"(Elias) has the reader on the edge of the seat till the end."— *Stringendo Magazine* for *Playing with Fire*

"This is a very deftly written murder mystery…and guaranteed to please this magazine's readership."—*The Strad* Magazine for *Spring Break*

"…fast-paced and punchily written…"—*Library Journal* for *Death and the Maiden*

I

UTOPIA RAISED

Chapter One

The letter Layton Stolz has been awaiting for weeks, months, his whole lifetime in a way, is in his trembling hands. It was in his mailbox when he returned home from work, tucked innocuously among the bills and the circulars and the endless requests for donations from the nonprofits. Because the skies were still darkening before five o'clock, he couldn't see who the letter was from until he was inside. Now, seated at his kitchen table covered by a green and white plaid tablecloth, which is in turn covered in clear plastic to prevent staining, he rubs the envelope between his thumbs and index fingers. Quality paper. High fiber content. None of that bright white, glossy stuff you get with junk mail. Those come-ons that scare you into extending your car warranty or for garden pavers made of cement that are supposed to look like real stone. Or for window blinds that will save you fifty percent off your energy bills. False advertising, really. No, this is the real thing. A real letter. His name and address have been typed out by a quality machine, he can tell that. The ink didn't bleed a bit. And the return address, embossed. High class. Official.

Office of Admissions
The Juilliard School of Music
60 Lincoln Center Plaza
New York, NY 10023.

Stolz doesn't open the letter right away. Savor the moment. Savor the moment. He mentally prepares himself for the disappointment for which he is in store, for sure. Maybe that's the real reason he puts off opening it.

He is eight-years-old again, at his Aunt Irma and Uncle Cy's rambling old house for Christmas. The biggest present under the tree is for him. He knows this because the night before, after everyone else had gone to sleep after stuffing themselves on ham and on sweet potato pie, he sneaked down and checked the card. "To Layton, from Santa." Yes, to Layton! Since Thanksgiving, he has been praying every night for an Erector set. What else could it be? It had to be the Erector set. He had personally written a heartfelt letter to Santa requesting it. It was just the right size, and it was for him! When, on Christmas morning, in front of his entire family he rips off the wrapping paper of smiling snowmen and tears apart the cardboard box, he discovers Santa has bestowed upon him a pair of new hypoallergenic pillows covered with lollipop-patterned pillowcases. "We hope you'll like them," Aunt Irma says, beaming.

But that was then and this is now. Stolz puts the letter down on the table, restraightens the stainless steel place setting for the third time that doesn't need restraightening, and sips coffee that had become lukewarm fifteen minutes ago. That's how long he has been staring at the envelope, divining its contents. He goes to the sink and washes his hands, again, until his stubby fingers are pink, then wipes them dry with a paper towel. He doesn't want to stain the letter, he tells himself. It could be something he might want to frame. For posterity. Wishful thinking. He knows the chances of being accepted to Juilliard aren't great, infinitesimal to be honest, but isn't today February 22, the anniversary of the Miracle on Ice? When those American college kids, still wet between the ears, beat the unbeatable Russian hockey team at the Olympics? "Do you believe in miracles?" that TV commentator cried. Why not? Anything's possible. At least, that's what Layton's mother had told him.

On his application, where they had asked about his musical experience, he had been brutally honest. He had been taught to always tell the truth. "No

4

fibbing now, Lonny," his mother used to say," using his nickname that was Lonny for a reason never known to anyone. Well, maybe he had padded his resumé, but just a bit. Clarinet lessons through the Flora Junior High School music program. Fightin' Bisons marching band for two years in high school.

Answering the essay question "What makes you passionate about music?" he wrote that he had most likely gotten his musical talent from his mother, Vivian, and had loved music ever since he could remember. Vivian had learned piano by ear and had been known locally for her light touch, especially with Scott Joplin ragtime, which she played in an understated fashion, not banged out as you so often hear. Even after going blind in old age, she continued for a time to perform at local senior centers to entertain the "old folks," as she called them, who responded warmly to her efforts.

Stolz's father, Douglas, hadn't shared those sentiments. He thought music was a waste of time. Whenever there was a family gathering where his mother was encouraged to play, Doug would try to talk them out of it. "It's a broken record." "Same old." "The Broncos are on TV." Usually, though, his efforts to influence others, like most else in his life, ended in failure, and he had to sit and listen along with everyone else. But after a few minutes, his body would twitch like a hound in hunting season, sending a clear message of his compulsion to be unleashed. Usually he'd be fantasizing, not about gamboling through the woods with a ruffed grouse between drooling jaws, but about the upcoming Wednesday night bowling league where he'd swill Coors with his factory buddies. For it was at Valley Mall Lanes where Doug Stolz fancied himself a hero, his exposed butt crack frozen in space as he posed like a Heisman Trophy, willing his iridescent blue bowling ball, as it spun down the lane, to convert that 8-10 split. Few things in life were as rewarding as the hollow clash of a bowling ball, barreling forward at eighteen miles per hour, colliding with rock maple pins. Doug had wanted his son to follow in his footsteps, to be the athlete he imagined himself to be in his mind's eye.

But Layton was unlike his father in every way, except that somehow he too ended up as a welder at Johnson's Machine Shop on Asbury Avenue. But he vowed he wouldn't die there, as his father had. Doug Stolz's life had ended at the machine shop in an accident, some suggesting with polite circumspection that Doug might have been inebriated when he neglected to don his welding helmet and his acetylene torch blew up in his face. After the funeral, Vivian Stolz sat at their living room piano and played Joplin's introspective rag, *Solace*, for the friends and family that came to pay their respects. Layton didn't know whether she played out of sincere sentiment or out of posthumous spite. If his mother hadn't had such an innately sweet disposition, he would have guessed the latter. But whatever the motivation, Layton was determined not to suffer his father's fate. Layton had a far different future in mind. Layton wanted to become an orchestra conductor.

A burly man with hairy Popeye arms, Layton was physically more suited for his job as a welder than as the maestro of a symphony orchestra, but what's inside a human soul isn't necessarily reflected on his exterior. Or inside a dog, for that matter. When Layton was a boy, Mr. Bruce next door had a big, tiger-striped Great Dane named Duke that was so tall it could lick Layton's face without having to stand on its hind legs. It was the gentlest dog in the world. Unlike the cute miniature poodle that bit Layton in the leg, drawing blood, and requiring his mother to take him to the ER for a rabies shot. From that experience, Layton learned to be wary of the superficial.

He had attempted to organize a student orchestra in Flora to further his musical ambitions, but there was no interest for intellectual, long-hair music in this small town where the western plains butted up against the Rockies. Flora High has a band and a glee club, the school board told him, as if he didn't know. Why would we need an orchestra? The one time he was able to patch together enough brave souls to perform *Greensleeves* at a school Christmas assembly, the boys carrying violin cases were targeted by the school jocks, pushed around, and told they were sissies. "Flora's values are not reflected in pussy music," one board member bluntly told him. The orchestra disbanded after the performance. That seemed to bring the matter to an end.

The setback didn't deter Stolz from continuing to love classical music, however. When he was at work he had the FM radio station turned on all day, much to the displeasure of his coworkers, who preferred country western, or even silence, to Brahms or Corelli. But Stolz was the most efficient welder and the most conscientious worker in the shop, polishing his tools and scouring his workspace every day, so they generally let him be. And it wasn't as if they could hear all that much, anyway, through the constant din of their labors.

One Tuesday, while Stolz was welding girder components for a trestle support at the train station, bits and pieces of a musical composition he had never heard before snuck through all the banging and clanging. The end of the composition was the most exhilarating thing he had ever heard, but because of all the noise he couldn't hear the soft parts, or the name of the music. On his lunch break, Stolz called the radio station. The name of the piece was the *Egmont Overture*, the person at the station told him. "How do you spell that?" Stolz asked. "E-G-M-O-N-T. By Beethoven." He wrote it down.

That Saturday, his first day off since hearing the overture, Stolz went to the Flora Public Library, which had a meager classical music collection. They had more recordings of Andy Williams than Ralph Vaughan Williams. *Moon River* might be his mother's taste, but not his. Stolz methodically rifled through the card catalogue under Beethoven, then overture, then Egmont, and was disappointed but not surprised they didn't have it. He would next try the Bridger County Library, forty miles away, first detouring to Holloway's Doughnuts for the usual: one old-fashioned cruller, one chocolate cake doughnut, and a small coffee with two single-serve containers of half-and-half.

The helpful librarian at the county library showed him to a room where LPs were shelved and where you could sit with headphones to listen to music. She was the prototypical librarian, Stolz thought approvingly. What a librarian should look like. Pointy horn rim glasses, hair in a bun, white blouse buttoned up to her chin. Gray skirt, down to mid-calf. A few years older than he was, it looked like. Probably an old maid, too. They don't call them old maids anymore. What was it now? Spinster? Bachelorette? Whatever it was, he wouldn't be asking her.

The LPs were shelved in alphabetical order, first by composer, and then by the name of the record's major composition. So, for example, under Bach, cantatas were followed by concertos. It wasn't hard for him to find Beethoven between Bartok and Bernstein. Beethoven had the greatest number of LPs of any composer, but Stolz's anxiety grew when there was nothing under E for Egmont. He frantically pulled out one LP after another. He was up to S for Symphony and still nothing. Symphony No. 1 in C, Symphony No. 2 in D...What would he do if he couldn't find the *Egmont Overture* here? Putting that out of his mind for the moment, he continued. Symphony No. 3 in E-flat, *Eroica*. Symphony No. 4. On and on. Finally! The *Egmont Overture*, performed by Eugene Ormandy and the Philadelphia Orchestra. Since the overture itself was less than ten minutes long, it had been packaged with Beethoven's Ninth Symphony, which was an hour long. That's why he had had such a hard time finding it. Stolz felt as if he had found hidden, forbidden treasure, like the toy submarine he miraculously unearthed as a child digging in the sand at the beach in Los Angeles. It was the only time he had been to the ocean. His parents had taken him to California for a reason he never knew. He had had no idea what child had left the submarine there under the sand, or how long it had lain there—maybe the boy himself was buried there with it, a titillating image that gave Layton goosebumps even in the summer heat—but the important thing was, the submarine was now his.

Stolz had a turntable at home, but it was outdated, with an age-blunted needle that made everything hiss and speakers that made everything sound like sandpaper. So he decided to stay at the library and listen to the record there, which would also save him on gas money by avoiding a second trip to return it.

Stolz listened in rapture. He couldn't put in words why it excited him so, but he felt to the depths of his soul that this moment was going to be a turning point in his life. Before listening to the overture a second time, he read the program notes on the back of the record jacket. This overture had a real story. A real "program," as the notes said. It was not what was referred to as abstract music, based simply on its inner logic like so much classical music. The *Egmont* had "musical imagery," beginning with Beethoven's portrayal of a heavy Spanish *Sarabanda*, the heavy boot of tyranny on the necks of the Dutch people. Then it was about how the Dutch Count Egmont rallied his people to rebel against Spanish oppression. About how, just before the ending that had so thrilled Stolz, Beethoven composed a musical prayer for victory that preceded the battle. And then the breathtaking triumph! The joyful strings! The blazing brass! Stolz listened to the overture seven times, looking over his shoulder from time to time to make sure that no one might be thinking there was something wrong with him.

Stolz had known that Beethoven was deaf—everyone knew that—but he had never been aware that so much of his music was preoccupied with themes of liberty and freedom. The program notes told about how his third symphony had originally been dedicated to Napoleon, but that Beethoven tore up the dedication when Napoleon declared himself emperor and then renamed it *Eroica*, or *Heroic*. Then there was the famous, explosive fifth symphony, and the ninth symphony, calling for universal brotherhood. The plot of Beethoven's only opera, *Fidelio*, which he also later named *Leonora* after the heroine's name, was about the liberation of a political prisoner. And though it was his only opera, Beethoven composed at least four different overtures for it, one called *Fidelio*, three of them named *Leonora*. And in all those compositions—the symphonies, the overtures, the opera—the music always goes from turmoil and struggle to freedom and liberation. Every time.

Stolz checked out more records, too many to listen to at the library before it closed for the day. Lost in thought, he arrived home that evening and couldn't even remember having driven. All Sunday, Stolz listened to Beethoven. He didn't mow the lawn. He didn't vacuum the house or do the laundry or change the sheets on his bed. He didn't watch any television or pay the bills or balance his checkbook. He didn't even indulge in his most religious weekend ritual of washing his Ford Granada. He just listened, feeling such a kinship with Beethoven that it was as if the two of them were a single entity.

On Monday, he went back to work at the machine shop. He was so preoccupied that he paid little attention to his work and overheated one joint with his acetylene torch. Sparks flew and fire flared up. His thick glass visor saved him from injury, but in that moment Stolz had a vision that was even more incandescent than the flame. It was not a vision of the past. Of his father. It was a vision of the future with the soul of Beethoven inside his breast.

That was the night he had applied to Juilliard. And now he has the envelope in his stubby-fingered, hairy-knuckled hands, which he suddenly realizes haven't stopped trembling. *What the heck,* he tells himself. *It's just a letter. A letter can't hurt you.* He will not tear it open, like he had torn open the box of his Christmas pillows. That act had been rash, and he has convinced himself that if had waited patiently for his turn, like everyone else, and had opened the box in a civil manner, the outcome would have been entirely different. He would have had his Erector set. He knows that, logically, it wouldn't have made a difference how he opened the box, that what was in there was in there, but still, that's what he believes.

In the living room is an antique wooden breakfront that had belonged to Grandma Grace, his maternal grandmother. She had willed it to Layton, and he had spent many hours refinishing and polishing it and getting all the drawers to slide smoothly. One drawer contains various articles he rarely uses—a magnifying glass, an old sewing kit, shoeshine wax. Among the objects, he finds the silver letter opener—so tarnished, I need to do something about this—which had also belonged to Grandma—and returns to the kitchen. He picks up the envelope and carefully slits it down the side opposite the return address to avoid damaging it. He places the letter opener parallel to the knife on his place setting, pulls out the letter, and flattens it onto the table.

Dear Mr. Stolz,

Thank you so much for your interest in the Juilliard School of Music and its conducting program. As I'm sure you are aware, the rigorous training provided by the program prepares students for a lifelong career in an intensely competitive field.

In your application, your deep passion for music came through loud and clear. The world needs more people like you, Mr. Stolz, who appreciate the greatness of musical achievement throughout the centuries and those who are tasked to translate dots on a page into meaningful, and hopefully memorable, experiences.

One would wish there were enough opportunities to enable people like you to pursue your dream. However, with Juilliard's limited resources and financial capability, we only accept eight students annually into the conducting program. Given your almost total absence of musical training and the fact that you are already over thirty years old, we have determined to offer the positions to younger, more highly-trained students, who have a greater chance of flourishing in the field.

Sadly, then, we regret to inform you that we are unable to accept you into the program, but wish you the best in your future endeavors.

Sincerely,

It was signed by the dean of admissions.

Stolz returns to the breakfront and rummages through the drawer, finding at the bottom of it the cheap, nine-by-twelve framed photo of his father with his smirking friends at the Valley Mall Lanes. In the photo, his father hoists a gold-painted plastic trophy, and his friends pose with their shiny black bowling balls, poised as if they are about to release them down the lane. Stolz twists open the little nails holding the frame's cardboard backing in place and removes it. He then covers the photo of Doug Stolz with the letter from Juilliard and replaces the backing. In the kitchen he taps a nail into the wall next to a framed photo of his mother, Vivian, just above the table. That photo was taken during the brief, happy period of her life after his father died and before the onset of her dementia. In the photo, she is seated at a piano wearing a party dress. Stolz doesn't know whose party it was—there weren't all that many—or whose piano. But the photo caught his mother relaxed and smiling, perhaps because it was one of the rare times she was free to be herself. Stolz hangs the framed Juilliard rejection letter next to that photo, where he will see both every morning for the rest of his life.

There is a certain irony to the name, Prairie View Nursing Home. First of all, any view of a prairie the facility might once have had was now obliterated by twenty miles of suburban sprawl: strip malls with inexpensive ethnic restaurants, eight-lane freeways, and recently-constructed pop-up high-end residential communities. The second reason is that one of its residents, Vivian Stolz, has been blind for years, and so has no view of anything. She is now also totally deaf. So when Layton tells her about his letter from Juilliard, she has no idea her son is even sitting in a chair next to her bed, let alone any ability to comprehend what he is talking about. But he talks to her anyway, more for himself than for her. More to be able to say out loud what is weighing on his mind.

With claw-like hands, Vivian clutches at the top of her blanket with the desperate strength of Wile E. Coyote clinging to a precipice by his fingertips. Both of their endings—Vivian's and Wile E.'s—are inevitable. Her translucent white skin, pulled taut over her cheekbones and a face immobile as an alabaster statue but for a quivering lower lip, is the Jolly Roger skull from a toy pirate ship that terrified Stolz in his youth. He wonders what, if anything, is going on inside his mother's head, and as he relates his story of deflated great expectations, a second stream of thought crawls wormlike into his head. If he were to cover his mother's face with his hand for a minute, a minute-and-a-half at most, she would be gone, and it would probably be better for both of them. She would probably even be thankful. But of course he won't do that.

He kisses her on her forehead, promises to return next week, says good-bye, and replaces last week's flowers, now wilted, with a new bouquet and fresh water. Spring Medley they called it at the florist. He tries to arrange the bouquet in an artistic way, but fails. What difference does it make? Maybe his mother can at least still smell, he thinks. He drives his Granada to nearby Castleton State Forest and, carrying his father's shotgun, walks into the woods for about a mile on frozen, snow-covered ground. He stops when he's sure he is alone, blasts his gun at anything that moves, and goes home. He would not want to be late for work tomorrow morning.

Chapter Two

A majestic maple reigns over the backyard. The tree reminds little Layton of an elephant, with its deeply scored bark and a limb that curves upwards, just out of his reach, that curls gracefully, just like an elephant's trunk. Within his reach, at his eye level, is a wound in the trunk from where a branch had broken off over the winter and which oozes a gluey, sweet sap that drips down the bark. Layton, scraping it off with his fingernail, imagines it is the elephant's snot and after tasting it, inserts it into his nose. He then careens through his yard like the rogue bull elephants on Wild Kingdom.

Their postage-stamp backyard patio, lying in the maple's shadow, is hardly big enough to contain the chaise longue, picnic table, and barbecue grill that occupy it. As the tree grows, its roots begin to push up against the patio floor from underneath, sending a network of hairline cracks spreading through the cement. Doug Stolz's solution is typically simplistic. Get rid of the tree, using a handsaw to cut it down to a stump, and then digging the rest out by the roots so it won't grow back. As far as a strategy is concerned, it isn't so bad, at least in theory. In practice, the problem is that it is a big tree and he has a small saw, and with his six-day work week at the shop, felling the tree and removing the limbs takes half the summer and an untold number of six-packs. And then his shovel and pickax aren't much up to the task of removing the stump. The Stolzes' next door neighbor, Herman Lovejoy, has a pickup truck, and thoughtfully offers to throw a chain around the stump, hook it to his truck, and winch it out—"Just yank it out like a loose tooth"—which could easily be accomplished in less than an hour. But Doug

Stolz won't hear of it. He doesn't want to feel as if his hours of exhausting manual labor have been a waste of time or admit to someone else coming up with a better idea. And he doesn't want to admit to his nemesis, the tree, that he needs assistance to defeat it, so he tells Herman to mind his own business and goes back to hacking at the stump with his shovel and pickax. Ultimately, Stolz manages to dislodge the stump, ripping its final resisting roots from their tenacious toeholds. And perhaps as a perverse testament to his victory, Stolz leaves the stump to rot on the ground next to the patio and refuses to allow anyone to remove it, though he does fill the yawning cavity in the ground with dirt and with the Winston butts and empty beer cans that are a statistical testament to the extent of his labors. All along, little Layton has watched his friend, the elephant, die, one piece at a time.

If there is one characteristic Layton inherited from his father, it is that dogged stubbornness. He understands getting into Juilliard had been a long shot. But even in the depths of his disappointment, he remains undeterred, convinced that the rejection will somehow spur him on to greater accomplishments. Where there's a will there's a way, his mother always told him. He has the will. All he needs is to find the way.

Every day, back on the job where he has worked since finishing high school, Layton ponders and plans. Because of his love for classical music, his co-workers have always given him a wide berth, as if he had a contagious disease or had registered with the Democratic Party. No one has any idea of what is going on in his head, and at first he doesn't, either. Months pass. Spring comes and goes. Summer comes and is almost gone, too, when on August 18 he calls the Bridger County Library and speaks to the librarian who had helped him find the recording of the Egmont Overture. That visit had been a turning point in his life, but apparently not in the librarian's, who needed a thorough refresher before she says, "Oh, yes, Mr. Stolz. Of course I remember now."

"Do you have the score to the *Egmont Overture* by any chance?" he asks, once the reintroduction is out of the way.

"I'm afraid we don't carry musical scores," she says. "Have you tried some of the universities? They might have what you need in their libraries."

Stolz hesitates, still smarting a half year after his rejection by an institution of higher learning. His silent vacillation must have been a dog whistle for the librarian.

"But I know of a music store in New York City that sells sheet music and scores," she says. "And at a discount, too, I believe. The Joseph Patelson Music House. It's a small shop, right in the shadow of Carnegie Hall they say, but I'm told lots of musicians buy their music there. I can get you their number if you want."

Stolz thanks the librarian and waits for the phone number. Before hanging up he asks her name. Just in case, of course. It's Smith. Ann Smith.

Stolz calls Patelson's. "Can you help me, please?" he asks. "Do you have the score to the *Egmont Overture*?"

"Which edition?" A bored young man's voice, the kind that sounds too busy to be bothered by people who don't know exactly what they want. Maybe he has other customers waiting or is in a hurry to go home. Or is that just the way New Yorkers talk?

"I don't know," Stolz says. "How many do you have?"

"We have five, sir."

Stolz is elated and also embarrassed. So much choice! But he has no idea about editions. He can't even name one music publisher let alone suggest which one he wants.

"Can you tell me what you've got?" he asks. "With the prices?"

In the end he orders the Eulenburg edition miniature score, under ten dollars. On the spur of the moment, he also splurges for a ream of music manuscript paper and a copy of *How to Conduct: A Do-It-Yourself Manual for Beginning Maestros*, by Gustav Müller, who Stolz is informed is an eminent conducting pedagogue. Stolz informs the pompous employee where he can go, but only after he hangs up.

Stolz immediately sets about rearranging his living room furniture to accommodate his project, moving any excess pieces into the garage and basement, and setting up a simple wooden table in the exact middle of the room that will be exclusively dedicated to copying by hand all the individual parts from the score onto the music paper. On the left side of the table will be the Beethoven score. On the right, the ream of paper. In the middle, the particular part he will be copying, behind which is a glass jar of pencils. Next to the jar are a pencil sharpener and erasers. Behind the jar, a desk lamp clamped to the back of the table. Behind the score, in the far left corner, is a cardboard box in which he will place the finished copied parts. And yes, oh yes, the Scotch tape to bind the parts.Can't forget that. Every item is precisely parallel or perpendicular to the other and to the sides of the table, which are parallel to the sides of the room.

A week later, upon returning home from work, the awaited parcel is sitting on his front doorstep. After a can of beef stew, he goes to work. Night after night, he allows himself four hours of sleep before getting ready for work at the machine shop. He has calculated he has to maintain that rigorous schedule because he has to finish the project before the school board meeting on September 7. That is part of his plan.

He hadn't realized what a chore copying the short *Egmont Overture* would be. There are so many different parts: two flutes, two oboes, two clarinets, two bassoons, four horns, two trumpets, timpani, first violins, second violins, violas, cellos, and basses. At his welding job, he was often bone tired by the end of the day, but he found copying the music was even more exhausting than that. After an hour, his hands inevitably began to cramp, reminding him of his mother's claws. He is constantly sharpening pencils by hand, the twisting motion aggravating an old wrist injury he had all but forgotten about, from when he slipped and fell on a slick shop floor that, unbeknownst to him, had just been mopped. Working through the night in the poor light of his desk lamp, his eyes have become so strained they burn as if his acetylene torch had been pointed at them.

When Stolz isn't too fatigued after his nocturnal bouts of copying, he stands in front of the mirror that hangs on the door of his bedroom closet. This isn't to admire how he looks, which he'd never consider doing even on his best days. Rather, it is to practice his conducting. He would read a chapter of Müller's book, look at a musical passage in the *Egmont Overture*, and stand in front of the mirror, conducting according to Müller's instructions with the optimistic hope that he is hearing the music correctly in his head. He tries to

16

revive the image in his head, vaguely recalled from childhood, of once seeing Leonard Bernstein conduct a *Young People's Concert* on television. Those expressive faces Bernstein made, sometimes ecstatic, other times snarling. The grand gestures. His arms raised high over his head. The prayerful poses. Leaping up at the big climaxes with his feet lifting off the podium like a Saturn rocket. Stolz practices all these moves. Lean forward, hands on the heart. Imploring: "Violas, more passion! More passion!" Roll your eyes back into your head, like you're in a trance. *Oops!* Can't see that one in the mirror. A cautionary hand up, like a traffic cop: "Trumpets! Shush! You'll drown out the clarinet." Of course, it will all look better when I'm not in my boxers.

Chapter Three

Stolz hasn't been in a school cafeteria for a long time. The odor of breaded veal patties and overcooked string beans, ghosts of school lunches past. The fluorescent lights, buzzing like a swarm of distant hornets. On the underside of the long Formica tables the Jackson Pollocks of fossilized chewing gum. Things haven't changed much.

The only thing out of place in the cafeteria are these adults. Sitting awkwardly at the tables, their haunches overflowing spindly plastic chairs, they're jumbo-sized eggs in a medium Grade A carton. It's hard to imagine these grownups had ever been children. They're dressed up, the men in ties and jackets, the women in dresses, as if doing so would lend the proper gravitas to this school board meeting. *We take our obligations as board members seriously. We don't receive a dime for our time. We come here at night after work, carving precious minutes out of our busy schedules. Because we are concerned about the future of education at Flora. For our children. For the community. We furrow our brows and make longwinded speeches about our concern because we are so concerned.*

Stolz looks at his watch. It is 7:15. The secretary is almost finished reciting the minutes and old business from the previous meeting. The most pressing items had been budgeting for new tarmac on the playground, and how to effectively prevent the student newspaper, *The Bullhorn*, from using the word homosexual without violating their first amendment rights. *Motion to table. Seconded. All in favor? So moved.* Stolz is the last agenda item of new business. First, there will be a discussion of whether to hire two or four new senior citizen safety patrol volunteers. Two of the old ones had departed over the

18

summer, one dying from old age, the other moving to Denver to take a job in lawn mower repair. *Do we have a motion we'll miss them? So moved? Seconded. All in favor? Unanimous? So do we just replace them or replace them and hire two additional? Safety of our children. In the budget? Will we have to order more belts and badges?*

Then a discussion of the school mascot, Mo, the Fightin' Bison. *He is tame, isn't he? Mo's a her. Is there such a thing as a female bison? There's no such thing as a tame bison. That's not the issue: some say it's cruelty to animals to have him...her...tethered up during football games. She can get spooked. Public safety. You're all just so PC. C'mon! Don't we have more important things to worry about? Tabled.*

With the undercard out of the way comes the main event everyone has been waiting for, a special presentation by Phillip Valentine, Under Secretary of the United States Department of Education. Valentine is a wiry built, thirty-something with the remnants of boyhood freckles and a shock of red hair. He has a nose that was big to begin with, but which was made even larger when it was broken in a bar brawl when he was fifteen. When he ran for New York City Council, his opponents mocked him for that nose, but he turned the tables on his detractors, campaigning with the slogan, "a nose for success."

Valentine is on a goodwill mission to Flora, doing a face-to-face with school boards throughout the land to roll out new curriculum guidelines that schools will be compelled to follow in order to continue to receive federal funding. The result of tough Congressional bargaining, the compromise provides "something for everyone." At least, that's how Valentine has planned on pitching it. He doesn't expect it will be a tough sell. Having grown up in the Hell's Kitchen neighborhood on Manhattan's west side, he spent more time getting his education on the streets than in the classroom, and had toughened his cojones even further through years of internecine warfare while serving on the New York City Council. Where he'd been born and bred, being stabbed in the back really did mean being stabbed in the back. Meeting with these Midwest yokels will be a piece of cake.

Except tonight he is meeting with resistance. The Flora school board isn't buying what he is selling. Okay, they say, you want us to try to improve test scores? We can live with that. But sex education? English as a second language? Black history? We don't have one black kid in our high school. Why do we need black history?

If Layton Stolz had been a betting man, he would have lost a lot of money thinking that Valentine would not be able to sustain his benevolent smile while being tarred and feathered. But it is clear Flora is not the first hostile community he has faced. He has a counter ready for every attack. *You make a good point, but think of it this way. Talk to me why this is important to you. We are as concerned about your children's education as you are. That's why...*

For his part, Stolz tries to concentrate on the presentation he will give after the board finishes eviscerating Valentine. *I have a feeling the board will not be in a receptive mood,* he thinks.

So Stolz imagines he is Valentine, smiling and explaining, squinting his eyes in deep thought, tapping his pencil on the table and looking up at the ceiling as he considers seriously, staying on the moral high ground regardless of the lances trying to prick him off it. *Why does Flora need to have an orchestra?* Stolz asks himself rhetorically. *And why should I, Layton Stolz, conduct it? Why should we rehearse the Egmont Overture by Beethoven all year and perform it at graduation?* Over the past week he has carefully printed all those questions, and more, on the front of index cards. On the back, he has written the answers, which he memorized. He stacked the index cards in a pile, closed his eyes, and pulled them out randomly, practicing his answers until they sounded natural and assured.

Classical music improves test scores. Here's the data... Playing in an orchestra helps develop social skills and positive attitudes to cooperation that will be valuable in future employment. Playing in an orchestra provides a safe, crime-free environment. The positive work habits. The cross-curricular discipline. He has it all down pat, and while Valentine continues to get skewered like shish kebab, he recites his thesis in his head. He will be ready. How can such a reasonable request be rejected?

Stolz isn't surprised that the meeting is far behind schedule. He had been slated to make his presentation from 8:15-8:30, after which the meeting would be adjourned. It is 8:47 when Valentine thanks the board for their kind attention, cheerfully reminding them that, if they do not embrace the new regulations, they will forfeit $100,000 in funding. Annually. Ballpark.

"Layton, it's been a long day, and we'd like to get home to our families," says Wayne Charsky, the school board chairman. Wayne is a construction engineer for Glenco Development, a big California firm that designs shopping malls, with an office in Fort Collins, leaving Wayne with a long daily commute. Wayne, whose son, Gus, was quarterback of the Fightin' Bisons football team, was the gentleman who had referred to "Greensleeves" as pussy music. "Can this wait until our next meeting?"

"What if I make it quick?" Stolz asks. He has started mentally rearranging his talking points.

Charsky looks at the other officers of the board for guidance. They all shrug.

"Okay, Layton. Five minutes," Charsky says, with the grave magnanimity of a governor pardoning a death row convict.

Stolz begins his presentation.

"How many of you have heard the *Egmont Overture* by Beethoven?"

"You mean egg *head* overture?" Wayne Charsky asks. John Thomas, a real estate broker and pit bull breeder in his spare time, lets out a chortle. Apparently he thinks this is funny, or he is grooming Charsky for a future real estate deal.

"Well, if you haven't heard of Egmont," Stolz asks, "how many of you might have heard of Beethoven?" This is supposed to be a joke, but he might as well have told one of his father's favorites to a funeral gathering: *You hear about the guy who had a heart attack and was asked, 'Are you comfortable?' 'I make a good living.'* His father's chest would rumble and he'd cough up phlegm even after the hundredth time he told it. Stolz wishes he had inherited his father's cockiness. He can barely force himself to smile. No one else bothers to.

"This is why I think the school board should consider having a student orchestra perform..."

John Thomas shuffles his pile of papers and begins tapping them on the table, stacking them into a neat rectangle. Laura Germaine, who has a child each in elementary, middle, and high school, takes a prolonged glance at her watch. Fred what's-his-name stands up and starts to put his coat on.

Doug Stolz survived for three days after his machine shop accident. Layton visited him at the hospital the day before he died, more out of the sense of guilt he would have felt had he not gone than out of love or sympathy.

The elder Stolz lay immobilized in his bed. Except for his mouth, for which he has lost his lips to the fire, his head is entirely wrapped in bandages. The surgeons had attempted unsuccessfully to save his eyes. When Layton sees his dying father, pity overwhelms him. He senses this will be their last time together. Sitting at his father's bedside, bawling his eyes out, Layton relates his deepest hopes and dreams, of his passion for music and his determination to be the best musician he can be. He would study, he would practice, he would go to a great conservatory. His father will be proud of him. When he finishes saying all he has to say, he feels a bond has been created that had never been there before. He is profoundly sorry it hadn't happened sooner, but at least now his father will die knowing his son loved him.

A sound emerges from Doug Stolz's mouth. It is more animal than human, and Layton isn't even sure whether it is intentional until it is repeated. Yes, it sounds as if Doug wants to say—needs to say—something. Layton leans over his father's bandaged head.

"I'm listening, Dad," he says. "Tell me."

With great effort, Doug says something. Without lips, in his weakened condition, it is unintelligible. Layton, certain this will be the last thing his father will ever say to him, asks if he could repeat it slowly so he can understand.

Doug lifts his head an inch or two off his pillow.

"I…said…you…will…never…amount…to…anything." Panting from the effort, his head falls back onto his pillow.

Layton returns to his chair. A few minutes later a nurse enters.

"Just checkin' on your Dad's numbers," she says cheerily.

Layton gets up and leaves. Doug Stolz died the next day.

"That bastard!" Stolz hollers, conjuring his dead father's voice in his heyday, before the fatal accident. It is a moment of inspired clarity, which he would come to understand is his unique gift, but which would ultimately become his downfall. For now, though, the example of his father, the father who had predicted his failure, will open the door to his success. He can see the door swinging wide open on well-lubricated hinges with the touch of his fingertip. A door that had always been there but one which until now had always been locked shut.

Everyone looks up at him. He has their attention, anyway.

"What bastard?" Wayne Charsky asks, no doubt thinking he is the intended target.

"That bastard, Phillip Valentine!" Stolz slaps his hand hard on the cafeteria table and jumps up to his feet. "Have you ever heard anything like that, my friends? Have you ever heard anything so repugnant? Can you think of a better example of federal government overreach? Or *worse* example, I should say? Are we gonna let those damned New York bureaucrats in Washington, D.C. *dictate* to us how to run our schools? Well, are we?"

"What's that got to do with egg head?" Charsky asks.

"I'll tell you what it's got to do with, Wayne. I'll tell you. The *Egmont Overture*, Wayne, is about fighting for liberty from a tyrannical central government. It's about *the people* being free to choose their own way of life. Their own destiny. It's about sloughing off an oppressive regime. Heck, there's even a prayer, a *Christian* prayer before the folks go into battle. And you know what, Wayne? The Dutch people kick Spanish ass! It's what America's all about!"

Fred what's-his-name sits back down.

John Thomas asks, "Be that as it may, Layton, we've got a cost factor here. What about the music expense? That's gotta cost an arm and a leg."

Index Card #19. Stolz opens the clasps of the tan leather brief case from high school days, the one that his classmates used to call him a nerd for carrying, and pulls out an armful of music.

"Exhibit A, John. It's all here," he says. "And ready to go."

"When are you going to practice, though?" Laura Germaine asks. "My children's schedules are already so full."

Index Card #8. "Every Saturday morning from eight to ten. It's free time.

No classes. No football practice. No band. September through June. We'll perform at graduation."

"Sorry, Layton," John Thomas says. "The band plays *Pomp and Circumstance* at graduation. Always have, always will. It's tradition."

Everyone on the board smiles, like a litter of conspiring Cheshire cats. They have outsmarted him. Good try, Layton Stolz. Close but no cigar. *Pomp and Circumstance* is American as apple pie.

Stolz smiles wistfully, shaking his head, like his own first grade teacher, Doris Seuringer, had shaken hers so many years ago. "What do you get when you rub your two hands together?" Miss Seuringer asks. It is a science question, about friction. The correct, intended answer to the little experiment, Layton was to find out too late, is heat. But how does six-year-old Layton Stolz know that? He rubs his hands together and is the first one to raise his hand with the answer because Miss Seuringer is his first love and he'll do anything to impress her. Miss Seuringer spots his wildly swinging arms and calls on him. "Yes, Layton? Can you tell the class what you got when you rubbed your two hands together?" "Dirt," little Layton says.

Hence, his head shaking. Good try, John, but you stepped in it this time. The correct answer is not dirt.

Index Card #23. "Ladies and gentlemen of the board," Stolz says. "Who wrote *Pomp and Circumstance*? I'll tell you. Edward Elgar. A Brit! A Victorian Brit! What is *Pomp and Circumstance* about? It is about monarchy. It is about empire. The English empire, the very enemy we fought against to win our independence. Egmont, on the other hand, is about freedom and liberty and independence, the very issues the good people of Flora have been fighting for against the very likes of Phillip Valentine. It's about state's rights," he argues. "Local control. So no one can tell us how to raise our kids." He says it again slowly for effect. "No one."

One baffled board member mutters, "Beethoven's about local control?" But the rest of the board is listening to Layton Stolz, and seems to be swayed.

Before they can rebound, he improvises. This is not one of the index cards. This will be the coup grâce of his inspiration. He says, "I need volunteers to bring doughnuts to the rehearsals. Hands up to bring the doughnuts?"

Three moms' hands shoot up.

"Hold on a second," Charsky says. "You're leaving out one small detail."

"What's that?"

"We don't even have an orchestra."

"If I take care of that," Stolz says, "do we have a deal?"

All eyes on Wayne Charsky. It really is getting late.

"Any objections? No? Okay. So moved. Meeting adjourned."

Chapter Four

The next morning, during his morning coffee break, Stolz calls the librarian, Ann Smith, at the Bridger County Library. He realizes it will be a long shot. He wants fifty copies of the recording of the *Egmont Overture* to offer the students as an incentive to join his new orchestra. Once they join, he'll require them to listen to it every day in order to be able to internalize what the music is supposed to ideally sound like, and therefore, theoretically at least, to play it better. Stolz has personal precedent for thinking the listening regimen will be an effective strategy.

It is nine-thirty on Saturday morning. The Lone Ranger has once again triumphed over his adversaries without having to divulge his identity behind his mask. Little Layton goes outside to play cowboys and Indians with his best friend and next door neighbor, Eddie. They both chant the show's theme music—*duh-duh-dup, duh-duh-dup, duh-duh-dup-dup-dup*—as they gallop about on imaginary horses, shooting at each other with their toy six-shooters. "I got you." "No, you missed me." "It's only a flesh wound." Years later, when his music teacher, Sue Giddings, informs him the music is the overture to the opera, *William Tell,* by the nineteenth-century Italian composer, Gioachino Rossini, Layton says, "No, it's not. It's the Lone Ranger." But whatever its name, because he has listened to it so often, he plays it on his clarinet better than anything else on the marching band's halftime playlist at Fightin' Bisons football games. As if he had played it all his life, because in a way, he had.

"I'm afraid we don't have record copying capability here at the library,"

Ann Smith says, "especially so many copies. But have you tried Sam Goody?"

"Who's he?"

"It's not a who," Ann Smith laughs. It's not a belittling laugh, though. It is light and birdlike. Stolz doesn't mind it. It's the first time he's ever heard her laugh. "Sam Goody is a what. They're one of the biggest record dealers in the country and I think they have an outlet in Denver. Maybe they would donate some records as a community service."

Stolz thanks Ann Smith for her advice.

"My pleasure," she says. "And if you need to call me after hours about anything, let me give you my home phone number."

Stolz takes Ann Smith's suggestion and runs with it. The Yellow Pages lists a Sam Goody at the Cherry Creek Mall. He calls and asks to speak to the manager, whose name is Leonard Brower, explaining what he needs and why. And, he adds, if Sam Goody could help out he would certainly encourage everyone in the community to patronize the store. Brower tells Stolz that reaching out to the community is what Sam Goody is all about, but as much as he'd like to be of assistance, the problem is he doesn't even have one copy of the *Egmont Overture* on his shelves, let alone fifty. Stolz senses he could be at a dead end. Yet he wants to forge ahead, but how? Using Doug Stolz's voice worked once, but this was clearly not the time to try it again. He simply could think of nothing to say, and so merely holds the phone to his ear. And waits. If nothing else, at least he will not be the first to hang up.

"What I would be able to do," Brower finally says, "is put in an order for twenty-five copies at our central distribution warehouse and have it delivered within a week. Would that be acceptable?" Half an Erector set would have been a lot better than none at all, Stolz thinks. Yes, it is acceptable.

Among the twelve-hundred students at Flora High, Stolz coaxes the handful of string players—eight violins, one viola, three cellos, and four string basses—into returning to the fold, with the promise that this time things will be different. He will make sure they'll be treated with respect and won't be bullied or badgered. And of course there are the free records and a promise of a year of free doughnuts. But since the *Egmont* also requires woodwinds, brass, and percussion in addition to string players, Stolz has to cajole some of the kids in the school band to join the group, promising them, in addition to the same benefits offered the string players, they could continue to play as loudly as they want. For any orchestral parts that still remained unfilled, Stolz has sweet-talked the elderly Sue Giddings out of retirement in order to fill in on piano.

It isn't supposed to be like this. Yes, it is only the first rehearsal, and, recalling the trauma of the Christmas pillows, Stolz has kept his expectations as low as possible. But he hasn't anticipated they can't even get the first note right.

It had been Stolz's plan for the orchestra to read straight through the *Egmont Overture*, warts and all, and then go back and start working on details. That had been one of Müller's recommendations from *How to Conduct, Chapter Eight: The Professional Approach to Managing a Rehearsal*. Stolz has studied the Beethoven score in great detail and is confident he understands where the rough patches will be for the students. Where the string players might have a hard time playing together, where the rhythms are difficult to synchronize, where the wind players will need to play especially well in tune. The easiest moment, he is absolutely certain, the easiest part is the first note. Everyone plays the same note, a simple F-natural. Beethoven indicated it to be played *forte*, loudly, something the band students, at least, should have had no trouble with. And the note lasts for a whole measure with a *fermata*, which means its length is arbitrary, to be determined by the conductor. Him. He can choose to hold it as long as he wants. No one will have to do anything but play that single note and stop playing when he stops conducting.

When Stolz and his new volunteer assistant, Ann Smith, had arrived at the high school band room a half hour before the beginning of the Saturday morning rehearsal, they found it in a shambles. It had all the earmarks of a Friday afternoon jailbreak. The floor was strewn with music folders as varicolored as the autumn leaves outside, loose sheet music, candy wrappers, and plastic water bottles, not all of them empty. Huddles of music stands stood like caucusing penguins. Trombones and tubas dotted the landscape like brassy monuments to long-forgotten explorers.

Stolz feels the sting on his left cheek. The slap would burn forever. His

28

doting mother, Vivian, has always cleaned his bedroom, putting toys away in the tin bin with the sad clown face, making his bed, blankets tucked neatly under his pillows, hanging up his clean clothes, and depositing soiled shirts and pants, socks and underwear in the white wicker laundry hamper. The morning after celebrating his eighth birthday at a party featuring a chocolate cake decorated with candy sports cars, and with entertainment by a live clown (actually his Uncle Dave), Vivian says, "Lonny, now that you're a big boy, it's time for you to be cleaning up your room." Being a concept wholly unfamiliar to Lonny, he innocently replies, "But that's your job." With a swiftness Layton has never before seen from his mother in all his seven previous years, Vivian's delicate right hand, the right hand that floated daintily and with grace over the gentle syncopations of a Scott Joplin rag, eliciting friends' oohs and ahs—"Vivian, you should have been a professional"—strikes him on the left cheek, raising a welt that will be red for days but will remain permanently raw in his consciousness. "Your father may think I'm his servant, but I'll be damned if I'm going to be yours, too." That evening, Vivian Stolz makes little Lonny his favorite dessert treat, rice pudding with cinnamon. But from this day on, Layton Stolz will always clean his room. He is too afraid to do otherwise. Afraid of being hit. Afraid of losing his mother's love. Tidiness is his obsession. Disorder, like his fear of betrayal, is too painful to bear.

"I'll straighten up," Ann Smith said. "You go get ready. It's your big day." She arranged the music stands and chairs, and placed the music to Beethoven's *Egmont Overture* on each student's stand along with the recording, courtesy of Sam Goody.

The students arrived in slow, intermittent drips, like ketchup out of a Heinz jar, but Stolz felt that to establish himself as the leader it was necessary to set a good precedent and start on time, so he tuned the orchestra even though not everyone was there. Müller had instructed that in an orchestra, it was the designated job of the principal oboist to play an A for everyone to tune to, first for the winds and brass, then for the strings. However, the oboist had encountered some difficulty with her reed and the pitch that came out was only a vague approximation of an A. So Stolz asked Sue Giddings to play an A on the piano and had the orchestra tune to that. It would have been good if someone had tuned the piano beforehand, because it sounded as if that hadn't been the case for several years. So much for tuning the orchestra.

They are ready for the big moment: Beethoven's *Egmont*. Stolz tapped his baton on the podium to get everyone's attention and raised his arms in preparation. But when he lowered them to begin, just like he had done countless times in front of the mirror, precisely timed to the record, it was a disaster. Sue Giddings, overly conscientious, played too soon. The string players entered as raggedly as a wind-shredded flag. The woodwinds were seemingly incapable of coaxing anything other than random, avian squawks from their instruments. Stolz, determined to persevere, ignored the disarray, but by the time he raised his arms to indicate the fermata, any sound that had been produced, however distasteful, had long evaporated into silence. What frightens him the most is that the students seem not to have any idea whether what they have just done (or not done) is either good or bad.

Müller wrote in *Chapter Four: Leadership*, that in order to be a great conductor you had to exhibit optimism and confidence or the musicians would first lose interest, then heart, and would ultimately turn on the conductor, like a mutinous crew under an vacillating ship's captain. Better to go off course with purpose than to give uncertain commands. "Tahiti is...that way. I think."

So Stolz taps his baton on his music stand.

"Let's try that again," he says, with a smile. "This time, everybody, look at me." This was something else he had read. Eyes on the conductor. He will repeat his gestures exactly. This time they will understand and follow.

He raises his arms. Everyone's eyes are on him. But as he lowers his arms, the eyes of half of the students fall back to the music, and the result is no better than the first time. Worse, this time a creeping insolence seems to infiltrate the silence, like a recalcitrant teen ordered by his parents to mow the lawn when what he really wants to do is jam with his guitar friends.

Stolz can't accept that his lifetime dream, to be a great conductor, will be shattered after one note. He had asked the students to watch him but most of them had kept their eyes glued to the music. Even though it was only one

30

note!

He recalled the Broadway show from his youth, *The Music Man*, and how the main character, Harold Hill, in a similar predicament, developed the Think System, "where you don't have to bother with the notes," to get his charges in the River City student orchestra through difficult times. But Hill was a con artist, not a musician. Stolz will find a way with integrity, not gimmicks. The students will perform Beethoven, not *Seventy-six Trombones*. Surely, there must be a way.

The kids sit there, waiting. They start to talk to each other, ignoring him. Stolz has no idea what to do. The conducting book did not address what to do when things were not going well. It assumed everything would go right, like assembling the self-propelling lawnmower in his garage. Follow Steps A through T, a spark plug here, a wing nut there, pull the chord and you're in business.

Stolz has to do *something*. He decides to discard the written rules. Some Assembly Required, the religious text to which he has faithfully adhered, has failed him.

"Okay," he says. "I want all of you to play a note. Any note. As loud as you can. Start whenever you want. For as long as you can. Go ahead."

The noise is as horrendous as it is deafening. Whelps from the trumpeters that turn their faces red as September tomatoes. Hair-raising screeches out of the strings. Glass-shattering frequencies from the flutes. But at least it is a sound, and an enthusiastic one, and at least a few students smile. Those who don't, cover their ears.

"Okay," he says when the din descends to a level where his voice can be heard. "Now play any note you want, which means you don't have to look at the music, but start it when I bang my hand on the music stand."

The sound is no more palatable, but at least it begins to bear some semblance of being together, like his mother's church congregation standing for yet another hymn.

"Okay. Now we're going to work on playing the F in tune." Stolz instructs Miss Giddings to play her F on the piano with each and every student, one at a time, until the correct pitch is at least approximated by everyone. It takes almost an hour.

"Okay," he says, when that is finished. "Remember where the F is on your instrument, which means you don't have to look at the music, and remember how loudly you played before. In fact, everyone close your music. I'm now going to bang on the music stand again, so this time play your F with me, really loud. Okay?"

Except Layton Stolz fools them. He acts as if he is going to bang on his stand, but stops abruptly when his hands are an inch above it. Nevertheless, the orchestra responds as if he had, playing reasonably together, with full force, and with something that resembles an F. They hold on to the F for as long as Stolz keeps his hands wide open and they stop together when he suddenly clenches his fists.

"Yes!" shouts a kid from the back of the viola section. Everyone laughs. The embarrassed boy's face, hidden behind a mask of acne and disheveled long hair that covers his eyes—how could he even see the music? Stolz wonders—turns red as Stolz's own father's during one of his drunken tirades. Stolz decides that the boy's spontaneous eruption will receive neither scolding nor praise. That would have distracted from the message he wants the students to take home with them, the triumph of teamwork for the sound they had just created. There wasn't anything about teamwork in Müller's book, at least nothing that Stolz could remember, but it feels like it makes sense.

"Okay," Stolz says. "That's enough for today. Go home and listen to the record. Everybody. Every day." They had rehearsed only one note. But, Stolz tells himself, that one note was Beethoven's.

Stolz leaves the school by the side door while Ann Smith collects the music folders. On his way to the parking lot, he is intercepted by the student who had shouted, "Yes!" The boy drops the cigarette he has been smoking onto the tarmac and rubs it out with the toe of his shoe.

"Hey, Mr. Stolz," he says.

"Yes?"

"Sorry I was out of line in there. It was just. Well, I couldn't believe we did it!"

"No problem, son. What's your name?"

"Duane. Duane Sheely. I play viola."

"Yes, I know. I could see that. Well, keep up the good work."

"I'll try. Thanks."

Stolz begins to walk away. He stops and wheels around.

"And one more thing," Stolz says. "No more cigarettes."

"If you say so."

Except for Thanksgiving weekend and Christmas vacation, the orchestra rehearses every Saturday morning from eight to ten, from September to June. Stolz teaches the ragtag orchestra the *Egmont Overture* note by painful note. In the process, he devises an effective if unorthodox and idiosyncratic baton technique, like a Navy flag waver on an aircraft carrier, which he continuously refines in front of his bedroom mirror so that the nascent musicians can develop an understanding of exactly how and when to respond to aural and visual stimuli. Every gesture, every minute movement of any finger, every twitch, nod, or bend at the neck, waist, and knees means something specific. After each rehearsal, Duane Sheely peppers Stolz with questions about tempos, dynamics, phrasing, what gestures he thought were especially helpful. Little by little, Sheely, having kept his promise to quit smoking, becomes Stolz's devoted music assistant, as Ann Smith has become his administrative one.

There is another boy, a violin player, who catches Stolz's attention. He is a little smaller than the rest, but good-looking, almost pretty. He is always one of the first to show up for rehearsals. Never the very first, but there is no one else who consistently arrives before him. Almost as if he wants to demonstrate how conscientious he is but at the same time not wanting to show off.

The same with where the boy sits. Stolz never tells anyone in the string section where to sit. That issue would sort itself out. The better, bolder ones with innate leadership qualities sit up front, and the weaker, meeker, though not necessarily inferior ones gravitate toward the back. That's how he'd have wanted it anyway, even if he had been the one to decide.

But this boy chooses to sit near the back of the first violin section, always on the fourth or fifth stand, and seems to be happy with that position. Stolz keeps an eye on him, and concludes that the boy feels he's good enough to play the more difficult first violin part but is reluctant to be in a "show off" position farther up toward the concertmaster position in front, though it looks like he is good enough to be there. The boy is always well-dressed, smiles all the time—not a dumb smile but a genuine one—except when he is concentrating on the music, and seems to have an easy way with all the other students, an unusual skill for a teenager, who are so often inclined to congregate in self-selecting, exclusive clans.

And the boy always seems to be prepared, is attentive to Stolz's every instruction, and never seems to have a look of confusion or bewilderment, even when Stolz is explaining a more arcane point.

At intermission of one rehearsal Stolz asks Ann Smith the boy's name, which she tells him is Ballard Whitmore. He instructs her to bring the boy to his office after the rehearsal. His office is simply a practice room, separated from the band room by a soundproof glass door, with a table and a chair.

"We haven't met yet, son," Stolz says.

"No, sir."

"I've appreciated your attitude."

"Thank you. I've really enjoyed being part of the orchestra."

"What year are you?"

"A senior, sir."

"Senior? You look younger than that." Stolz smiles.

Whitmore smiles back.

"I suppose. That's what my Mom says, too."

"So you're off to college next year, then?"

"I'm going on my mission first, and then to BYU."

"Brigham Young? Mormon, are you?"

"Yes, sir."

"So, lots of brothers and sisters, I suppose?"

"Just sisters. Six of them, sir, and I'm the youngest. Sometimes I wonder what my parents would've done if I had been a girl."

"Now, there's a thought. Where's your mission, Ballard? Can you take your violin?"

Whitmore laughs.

"I don't know yet. And probably not. But soon as I get back I'll start practicing."

"Yes, I'm sure you will," Stolz says, even though he isn't. "Well, keep up the good work."

"Thanks, I will."

Then, for reasons he would never be able to adequately explain, and which he would only again think about years later, after he had gone to great lengths to have him imprisoned —"the boy left me no choice," he would insist—Stolz laid his hand on Ballard Whitmore's head. It was, for him, a rare spontaneous gesture, spontaneity not being a quality he either exhibited or even aspired to. Yet there it was. His hand was on the boy's head, and the boy was looking up at him, almost reverentially. Was this some sort of benediction? A religious rite? Was it a subliminal reference to some kind of Mormon thing of which he had only been vaguely aware? Was he being the kind of father he never had? The father he would have wanted his own to be? And was this boy the kind of son he wished he had been? Did he know—how could he know?—even then, that ultimately he would have to sacrifice this young man?

There is a knock on the glass door. It's Duane Sheely. Has young Duane watched this whole sequence? Stolz, quickly removing his hand, isn't sure and somehow feels guilty. He turns the hand motion into a gesture for Duane to enter.

"What can I do for you, Duane?" Stolz asks.

The boy seems tongue-tied, with Ballad Whitmore standing there, a witness.

"Is there a problem?" Stolz asks, trying to read the silence. Strange comrades, these two, he thinks.

"No," Duane says. "It's just...I wanted to know if..."

"If? If what?"

"Never mind."

This makes Stolz uncomfortable.

"Well," he says. "Let's get back to rehearsing, then."

Duane shrugs, and leaves without another word. Ballard Whitmore nods in Stolz's direction, a nod of thanks or perhaps understanding, Stolz thinks, and leaves.

As a condition of remaining in the orchestra, all students had to sign an agreement that they would listen to the LP of the *Egmont Overture* every day. Ten minutes long, once a day. That's all. After a while they're able to hear it in their sleep. Stolz exhorts them on relentlessly. "Just a little bit better every day! Just a little bit! You're getting there. Piccolo, you came in eight bars too soon! Go home and listen." When they come to the prayer section of the overture, he stops the orchestra and tells everyone to kneel down and pray, really pray, for the future of America, so they could sense what the desperate need to be liberated from oppression might feel like and to understand what was in Beethoven's heart. When they get to the victorious coda, representing the triumph of the rebellion, he has all the string players engage in a mock sword fight with their bows, shouting and cheering, while the brass and winds play their heads off. He begins to reward their efforts with hamburgers and milkshakes after every rehearsal, and when the mothers see how hard Stolz is working with their kids and how quickly his wallet is undoubtedly being drained, they graduate from doughnuts to potluck parties with homemade tuna noodle casserole and American chop suey.

The year progresses through football season, through basketball season, through baseball season. For the orchestra there is only one season: *Egmont* season. Thirty-nine two-hour rehearsals for a ten-minute piece of music. During the twenty-third rehearsal, Stolz suddenly becomes lightheaded and almost collapses on the podium. It isn't because the orchestra is failing. On the contrary, it is actually starting to sound a little bit like the recording. It isn't because he is ill, as, overall, he is convinced he's never felt more alive. But something is disturbing him that he isn't able to put his finger on, like trying to remember a dream that seemed so clear and cogent in the middle of the night but which was, upon awakening, just out of reach of recall. But that undefined something strikes him like a freight train, right there on the podium. *Egmont Overture—then what?* What will I do next year? Until that moment, he hadn't given the prospect of success a grain of thought. At that moment, the future is a vast vacuum. A black hole. If there is such a thing as amnesia of the future, he has it, and it causes him to panic. Stolz stops the orchestra in the middle of a phrase and clutches his music stand so he won't fall. The orchestra waits expectantly to be instructed what they were doing wrong, because by this point they have developed faith in Stolz's vision. But there is no chewing-out forthcoming. No admonition. No motivational talk. When he regains his breath, for the first and only time, Stolz ends a rehearsal early. Both Duane Sheely and Ann Smith, recognizing Stolz's distress, approach him as quickly as they can without alarming the students. They each take hold of one of his arms to help him off the podium.

"Duane," Ann Smith says, "Leave him to me. You and Ballard go put away the music."

Duane releases his grip on Stolz's arm, but not before looking at Ann Smith in a way that makes her shudder.

"What am I going to do, Mother?" His personal Sphinx, his mother. They said she was still alive, but he can't even tell if she is breathing. Stolz had driven distractedly from the school to the nursing home. On the way there a dry gale from the mountains blistered his car and almost rolled it off the freeway. He had pulled off onto the verge and cried in silence, less because he had just escaped death, more because he hadn't. Why is he bothering to talk to her? He might as well talk to a brick. Is he searching for guidance? Pretending to be the good son? Offering to exchange places? Yet, he talks and talks at her bedside, seeking answers to questions he can't even articulate. When he finishes saying everything he can think of saying, he replaces the faded bouquet on his mother's dresser, as always, with a new one. Hyacinths. It's almost spring and they smell powerfully, like dryer sheets. Mother always liked the smell of dryer sheets.

Stolz goes home. He turns on the television, but there's nothing more interesting than an infomercial about a food slicer-and-dicer that will change his life, and as much as he wants to change his life, he doesn't think the slicer-and-dicer will do the trick. Besides, he doesn't cook much anyway, so he turns it off.

He vacuums his living room carpet for the second time in the day, making sure the lines of the vacuum cleaner wheels remain parallel. Then, while a can of Campbell's chicken and rice soup simmers on his stove, he dials Ann Smith's number. He has a request.

"I'm sorry, Mr. Stolz, but you know the library is closed tomorrow. It's Sunday."

"It's my day off. You know it's hard for me to come any other day."

"Yes, but...Oh, I suppose I can open it. For an hour. Yes, I can do that."

On Sunday, Stolz drives the forty miles to the Bridger County Library and checks out an armful of records, promising to return them the next week.

"You keep them as long as you want," Ann Smith says, and, to seal the deal, extends her hand, which Stolz grasps awkwardly in order to avoid dropping the records. He will listen to these records daily, before going to work in the morning, for the next three months.

By the end of the school year, the entire town of Flora is buzzing, well aware what Layton Stolz has been doing with the students all those Saturday mornings. High school graduation, typically a stodgy school affair, has become a festive community celebration. For the occasion, Stolz has the orchestra festooned in the black and red of Flora High School's Fightin' Bisons marching band uniforms. At the performance, attended by the entire graduating class and their families, the faculty, and whoever they could fit into the auditorium, the student orchestra gives it their all. Someone with a trained ear might have commented that the cacophony verged on the ghastly, but the townsfolk are so roused by Beethoven's call to arms and so astonished by the sense of purpose demonstrated by the youngsters that it could have been Eugene Ormandy and the Philadelphia Orchestra, and if they had known the difference they wouldn't have cared. When it's over, the orchestra, deluged by a chorus of whoops and a standing ovation from the audience, beams with pride.

Layton Stolz, more determined than ever to pursue his destiny, does not let this opportunity slip by. After the graduation ceremony, there is a cheese and cracker reception in the same cafeteria where he began his crusade nine months earlier. In a style unnatural to him but fortified with renewed determination to succeed, he glad-hands each and every member of the school board, who pat him on the back and shake his hand and tell him they never thought in their whole lives they'd say they liked classical music.

By the time the school doors close for the evening, Stolz, exhausted, has elicited the board's blessing to incorporate the orchestra into Flora High's afterschool music program. They are likely under the impression that what Stolz has in mind is simply a rehash of the Egmont Overture each year for graduation. Though Stolz says nothing to dissuade them from that impression, this is not at all what he has in mind. The next morning, he submits an orchestra curriculum for the following five years that he had been working on from the day he brought home the stack of Beethoven LPs from the Bridger County Library:

1st year: *Egmont Overture*

2nd year: Third Symphony, *Eroica*

3rd year: Fifth Symphony

4th year: *Leonora* overtures (all four)

5th year: Ninth Symphony, *Ode to Joy*.

Though every one of those compositions carries the message of liberty, freedom, and brotherhood, there is a logical progression of difficulty, as Stolz sees it, from one piece to the next. Beginning in eighth grade, each of five orchestras will perform only the one designated composition and will rehearse the entire year for the performance, after which the students will move up to the next rung of the ladder. Stolz will have only two intractable rules: A student will graduate to the next level only if he or she attends every rehearsal, arriving on time, and comports her- or himself like a lady or gentleman. Stolz is instinctively sure that if the students adhere to those two rules, their playing will inevitably get better. And he is right.

As the years pass, his Beethoven Sequence, as he calls it, starts to attract some attention. After the first year, when the orchestra performed the *Egmont Overture* at graduation, school administrators noticed a blip in the test scores and overall attendance records of students who had enrolled in Stolz's orchestra. It was debated whether those outcomes were correlated to the Sequence. The empirical data teased intriguingly, but was by no means conclusive. But when those numbers continued to inch up from year to year as the five-year plan unfolded, it was hard to deny the conclusion that the phenomenon was indeed cause and effect. Not only did students' classroom attendance and grades soar, visits to the principal's office and school altercations plummeted. Kids actually started *wanting* to join the orchestra. It became a status symbol to be a Sequence kid. And the students in the orchestras adored Layton Stolz—he was not a rah-rah kind of mentor, but he never raised his voice, either—seeking him out after rehearsals for counseling on everything from preparing for exams to whether to ask so-and-so to the prom. His door was always open. Stolz came to be considered something of a local guru.

Layton Stolz never expected or even wanted to be a leader, at least in the sense of being a motivator or role model. He neither sought the spotlight nor basked in it. Certainly, in a way, a conductor was a leader. But even then, it was still the music that was the focal point. Now, people were coming to him with their cares and concerns, and not just the students. Not wanting to disappoint them, he would offer advice in as few words as he could muster. He didn't know whether it was good advice or bad advice, but they seemed to feel better after talking to him, so... What he really wished for was to simply rehearse Beethoven, then go home and be left alone. It now appeared that vision was illusory, and so he accepted the public limelight with as much grace as he was capable of.

Stolz had saved Beethoven's Symphony No. 9 for the fifth and final year of the Sequence. It was the epitome of Beethoven's deepest convictions about universal brotherhood, and it was also the most difficult symphony to stage, requiring an expanded orchestra, a chorus, and four vocal soloists. Its music was so taxing that he knew he would need professional singers for the roles. But by the time the fifth year rolled around, the Beethoven Sequence had become such a local phenomenon that all Stolz had to do was call Western Voices, Colorado's regional opera company. "What took you so long to call us?" they asked.

Chapter Five

It couldn't be helped. It was no one's fault. No one was to blame. Sometimes things just work out that way.

Those fatalistic sentiments didn't do anything to quell Phillip Valentine's raised dander. He doesn't believe in bad karma. He doesn't want to hear excuses.

"Have them change it," Valentine says. Recently appointed Deputy Secretary of the Interior, he is back in Flora, meeting with the city council and local environmental officials. It has been five years.

"They said they can't, sir," says his most courageous aide, Stewart Wolfe. Wolfe had been born wearing a suit, or so it had been said behind his back. Pasty-faced and prematurely pudgy, he is destined to be a right-hand man, loyal to a fault to anyone who appreciates his strongest quality, loyalty. He was lucky to have been spotted by Valentine when Wolfe was campaigning for a rival in the New York City Council. Wolfe disseminated lies and half-truths about Valentine through the rumor mill on a daily basis. Still, Valentine won, the rival lost, but Valentine, appreciating Wolfe's skill set, signed him up to do the same job for him. Wolfe was a remora to Valentine's shark, and the symbiotic relationship had worked to each other's benefit for years. Wolfe owned a nice ranch house with vinyl siding in Oyster Bay, Long Island, that came furnished with an attractive wife and two children. Wolfe would take a bullet for Phillip Valentine, or so he said.

"What you mean, 'they can't'?" Valentine groused.

"Our meeting was only scheduled last week. Their concert has been on their calendar all year. It's seems to be a big deal here, this Beethoven Ninth thing."

"Let them start it some other damn time."

"They say they can't," Wolfe says. "They've hired a chorus and four singers who they've paid to—"

"I don't want to hear about the damn singers, and we certainly can't change our meeting time. Didn't you tell me I have a plane to catch? Didn't you tell me I have to be in Albuquerque for a breakfast meeting with that idiot, Soplers?"

"Shall I cancel the breakfast with Congressman Soplers?"

"Don't you dare. The president says I need to kiss his ass to get the appropriations bill passed. Otherwise, I'd say yes. How Soplers got to be chair of anything more than the coffee room cleanup committee is beyond me."

"Yes, sir."

"Fuck it. We'll just have the damn meeting tonight as per schedule. Now that I think about it, maybe the fewer locals, the better."

Valentine is in town to inform the good citizens of Flora and neighboring communities of new conservation regulations to mitigate environmental degradation of nearby hundreds of thousands of acres of federally owned Bureau of Land Management territory. Whether they are aware of the new regulations or not, Florians' use of motorized vehicles on BLM land is now illegal. Since time immemorial, and certainly long before the land became federal property, they had been traversing these unpaved backroads and trails, first on foot, then on horseback, then in cars, and most recently with their ATVs. But times have changed. Local population has increased tenfold in the past fifty years. Outdoor recreation is skyrocketing even faster, with a corresponding threat to the health of wildlife, water quality, and riparian habitat. Certainly, reasonable people would understand the rationale for the new regulations, though they might not sympathize with them.

But forget the facts and figures, is Valentine's thought. He isn't a big fan of facts and figures. They like their football here in Flora, don't they? The Fightin' Bisons? Yes, that's their name. State champions three years running, isn't that what Wolfe told me? So talk about the new regulations like the new football rules. Penalties for late hits. Helmet to helmet. Protect the players. Common ground, there. Protect the environment. Safety first. Shit, you can still go onto the land. Just cut out the joyriding. Bicycles instead of motorbikes. Good for your health. It might just work.

What Phillip Valentine is not going to tell the people of Flora is that he doesn't give a damn about environmental concerns, theirs or Interior's. The closest he has ever come to a national park was the Bronx Zoo when his aunt dragged him there as a kid. He hated the outdoors. The rain and the mud, the mosquitos and all the bigger animals that could bite. They should all be in cages. If the locals turned forests into deserts with their ATVs, it meant fewer forest fires. Good news, right? Whatever, his raison d'être is simple: Please his boss, the president, because if he pleases the president, he'll get the president's support when it's his own turn to reach for the gold ring.

It's a typical summery evening on the eastern slope of the Rockies. Hot, dry, winds sweeping down off the mountains, nonstop sheet lightning taking over as the sun sets. A good chance of a violent thunderstorm. It is in the forecast, like it is almost every day this time of year.

When Valentine and his staff arrive at Town Hall at six-thirty there's already a boisterous crowd gathered on the lawn. At first he figures it's the usual lynch mob and considers having Wolfe call in for more police protection, but he doesn't notice any protesters with their ridiculous homemade signs spouting their constitutional rights, and when they open the doors to the building only a few people enter. What neither Valentine nor his staff are aware of is that Town Hall is next to the high school. The meeting and the Beethoven performance are both scheduled for seven o'clock. The crowd is there for the concert, not for his meeting.

It is the culmination of the first complete Beethoven Weekend, in which all five Sequence orchestras will have performed, from grades eight through twelve, with Layton Stolz conducting three concerts, Friday, Saturday, and Sunday evenings. The first combined the *Egmont Overture* with the *Eroica* Symphony. The second program included the *Leonora* overtures and the Fifth Symphony, and tonight, the grand climax will be the monumental Ninth Symphony. Leonard Brower from Sam Goody's is here, handing out discount coupons to anyone who'll take them. Goody's, having seen its statewide sales figures climb for the previous five years, mirroring the expansion of Layton Stolz's Beethoven Sequence program, is a major sponsor of the weekend, the company name prominently displayed on the programs. Musical instrument salespeople representing Yamaha, Baldwin, and other major instrument makers set up booths displaying their wares in the cafeteria, which has been converted into a makeshift mini-convention center. Parents organized parties before and after each concert. John Thomas set up a wood-fired smoker on the soccer field early in the morning to make his famous slow-cooked barbecued ribs. At four-thirty there was already a line. Laura Germain sold her to-die-for peanut butter cookies in the school lobby, donating the proceeds to the Sequence.

How big a crowd is it? Onstage there are the seventy-three members of the orchestra, and another hundred-four combined voices comprising the glee club of Flora High and the opera choir of Western Voices. Duane Sheely, who had played viola in the very first *Egmont Overture* performance, was so intent on being part of this historic event he returned to Flora to sing in the chorus. Helping fill the auditorium's one-thousand-one-hundred-fourteen sold-out seats were the musicians of the four younger Sequence orchestras. In attendance because their membership technically required them to be, the students had become so eager to be invested in the system that only a natural disaster would have prompted their absence. They imagined themselves onstage, basking in the glory of Beethoven's Symphony No. 9 when one day it would be their turn. So, yes, it is a big crowd, at least as far as the history of Flora is concerned. The biggest, in fact, easily topping the state championship football game against the Connorville Cougars three years earlier. Some curious music lovers have even come all the way from Denver and Fort Collins.

In the band room behind the stage, students, having once again donned the school's black and red, tune their instruments, though with the adrenaline flowing and everyone playing so loudly it is virtually impossible to hear themselves. For this special weekend Layton Stolz is wearing his black suit for only the second time, the first time having been at his mother's funeral.

"Your mother would have been proud of you," Ann Smith says to Stolz, off in a corner by the water fountain, which, irritatingly, is not functioning. His mouth is so dry. But he is as deaf as Beethoven to the cacophony surrounding him because he is running the entire one-hour score of the ninth symphony through his head. All those sudden tempo changes. He has to get them all right. It is so complex. Maybe he should go over it with the students one more time.

"What you've done—"

He interrupts her, more harshly than he meant to.

"My mother? What about my father?"

Not having a suitable answer, or even understanding the trajectory of his question, Ann Smith merely squeezes his hand a little harder. Stolz doesn't want the students see him holding hands with anyone, and pulls his away.

"I've got to go study the score again before the concert starts," he says, anxious to retreat to the principal's office, where he can shut the door and be alone.

"Of course."

Though the size of the contingent who showed up for Valentine's Town Hall meeting pales in comparison to those going to the concert, their sense of mission more than compensates for what they lack in numbers. They do not take kindly to Valentine's message of abstinence, to any degree, from land they consider their own, and harangue him with angry comments about federal intrusion and state's rights. Local reporters take furious notes, chopping at their pads with rough, penciled dashes to keep pace with all the expletives. Heated arguments are matched by the heated atmosphere. With the air conditioning shut off for the weekend, at both Town Hall and the high school, windows and doors are opened wide, like mouths agape. Like the Scream.

Next door, in the auditorium, the ambiance is as congenial as Town Hall's is contentious. In the five years since the first performance of the *Egmont Overture*, the skills of the students and of Layton Stolz have improved markedly. At first, like day-old foals, they'd wobbled on uncoordinated legs that threatened to collapse. But, like the foals, they somehow managed

46

to defy gravity and remain standing. And they learned to walk. And they learned to run. The students are not close to being thoroughbreds, but they are now at least able to pull a plow, and for the agrarian folks of Flora, that is as good as they need to be.

So when Stolz walks onto the stage and gestures for his student orchestra to rise, the ovation they receive has far greater meaning than beaming parents thinking, "I couldn't be prouder of my darling Britney." It is real excitement generated by real anticipation. They are going to experience some real music, the first performance of the Beethoven Ninth Symphony in the one-hundred-twenty-one-year history of incorporated Flora.

Over at Town Hall, through the open windows, they can hear the applause billowing from the auditorium, even over Martin Hargrove's diatribe about how the Department of Agriculture has been screwing him out of the farm subsidies they had promised, has decreased the tax deductible write-off for the loan interest on his farm machinery, and now "you're going to kick us off of land we've been freely using for the past hundred years? Let me tell you something, mister, the federal government doesn't have the right!"

Valentine replies by saying that Agriculture is not his department, but he would be happy to look into Hargrove's concerns. Getting back to his own issue, he explains that BLM land "belongs, in both a legal and philosophical sense, to all the people of our great country. We are stewards of the environment, and we ask you to join us in protecting the land for our children and grandchildren."

"You mean *your* children!" Brenda Ruzicka shouts. "Your rich *east coast* children!" Her point of view is vociferously reaffirmed by loud mumblings. If it had been a church congregation, they would have cried out, "Hallelujah!"

Over the years, Phillip Valentine has mastered the jargon of diplomacy. "Frank and direct" is how his office routinely refers to these types of exchanges. He is not shaken by this posse. He has learned how to take the heat. Part of his calculation is the run for the presidency that has long been in the back of his mind. He hasn't shared that thought with anyone, not even his wife, Greta, and their two teenage kids. Yet. This meeting tonight is a mere blip in the road, and if he plays his cards wisely, by the end of the meeting the townspeople here will say, "Well, shucks, we might not agree with the man, but at least he was honest." That is the best result he can expect. As long as they don't realize he doesn't give a shit about BLM land, he'll be okay.

The back-and-forth continues for another hour or so. The locals are taking no prisoners and refuse to even consider a moratorium on driving their ATVs on BLM land. Valentine is attacked as being a representative of "a godless bureaucracy." From time to time, some of the more declamatory phrases of Beethoven's Ninth leach from next door into their meeting, a surreal juxtaposition. Voices are raised to compete with the music.

Brenda Ruzicka stands. "Secretary Valentine, I think it's time for you to leave Flora. Right now. I wouldn't want to have to guarantee your safety."

Valentine's response happens to coincide with the climax of the symphony, when the entire orchestra and chorus give it all they've got. With all the windows open, Valentine's words can't clearly be heard above the music, even with his microphone. No one except Valentine will ever know what those words were. However, Beethoven's words are heard, and though no one there understands German, they have learned from Layton Stolz it has something to do with brotherhood, freedom, and/or liberty. Maybe even God. One by one they stand up and they sing along with the chorus next door. Not knowing a word of German, let alone the text, they substitute *"La-la la-la-la-la"* for *"freude schöner Götterfunken."* A small group sitting in the back of the town hall bursts out into a chant of "USA! USA!" and the Rocky Mountain thunder, which had considerately gone into abeyance for the bulk of the meeting, decides at that moment to resume in full force. Martin Hargrove, who had been one of Doug Stolz's bowling buddies, later said to his wife that the thunder was Doug rolling 300s in the great bowling alley in the sky, making amends for the son he didn't treat right in life. All combined, the din is more than sufficient to drown out whatever Valentine is trying to say, which is now so laced with profanity it is probably better for him he can't be heard. In the end, Valentine, red-faced, gives up and leaves with his aides and, as Brenda Ruzicka would later quip, with his tail hanging between his legs like a whupped mongrel. And, as it turned out, a very wet mongrel, as no sooner does Valentine leave the premises then it starts to rain cats and dogs.

Chapter Six

Layton Stolz can't sleep. It is still black as Hades outside and, though there are more than three hours until he has to be at work, a palpable anxiety, almost panic, precludes him from even closing his eyes again. It isn't the rainstorm that keeps him awake. That subsided hours ago. He quietly slides out of bed, not wanting to wake Ann Smith and have her witness his distress. He closes the bedroom door behind him and tiptoes downstairs to the kitchen, where he makes a cup of instant coffee and sits at the kitchen table, looking out the window into the darkness. A line of starlings perch on a dripping telephone wire, black against black in the predawn.

After the concert, his triumphant students had presented him with a full-size replica of the famous bust of Beethoven sculpted by Anton Dietrich, on display at the Vienna Opera House since the mid-nineteenth century. How can someone who chips away with a hammer and chisel and steel wool and whatever else they use, Stolz asked himself, duplicate the subtleties of someone's personality in a piece of rock? A little chip here. A little chip there. Polish this, gouge that and you end up with Beethoven? And those aspects of Beethoven so central to his temperament that Dietrich had managed to so perfectly etch in stone: pride of achievement against all odds, independence, love of freedom, virtue, vision. Power. Yes, all those things. That much was clear. But there was another side of Beethoven that Stolz had read about, which neither he nor the public chose to dwell on. Even the historians and musicians tiptoed around the issue, as he had tiptoed down the stairs, keeping things quiet. Keeping things hidden. Beethoven's dark side: the arrogant, antisocial, unkempt, miserly, litigious, unrepentant social-climbing, and some would say misogynistic, pandering money-grubber. What would Dietrich's bust of Beethoven have looked like if he had chosen those attributes to carve in stone instead of the heroic ones?

It isn't that Stolz is particularly concerned with stone statues. You drop them and they break. What troubles him is that his idol and his idol's music are not one and the same. One exists within the other, yes, but they are seemingly separate beings. How does one account for that? How is it possible the expressions of one's soul can be so counter to one's outward behavior? How could Jekyll, the genius, be Hyde, the man? It didn't make sense. Was it only Beethoven, though, who was a walking contradiction? Or is it everyone? Is it *him*? Layton Stolz, son of Vivian and Douglas Stolz. Stolz broods as he peers out the window, seeing, but not observing, the sky begin to lighten. Does the work he has been doing for the past five years—his Beethoven Sequence—represent *who he really is*? Or is the Sequence simply a fungal spore that he has injected into a cultural Petri dish, which has sprouted of its own accord, irrespective of who he really is. Maybe he's fooling himself. Maybe Layton Stolz is no different from Doug Stolz, Wednesday night bowler. Maybe he, Layton, is merely a welder in a factory that solders together pieces of metal for unnamed overpasses. Who, with his helmet on, looks just like every other welder. Like the starlings sitting on the telephone wire outside the kitchen window while he drinks instant coffee in the dark. They all look the same, hardly visible at all. He can hear them, though, whistling and clicking and chirping. In the dark.

Five years. In five years he has learned to conduct all of five pieces. (Okay, eight if you count the four Leonora overtures individually). A real conductor conducts five pieces every couple of weeks. What has he really accomplished? Anything? Might his new friends, Wayne Charsky, John Thomas, and Laura Germaine, have really been mocking him behind his back? *Let our little local genius have his fun. Just keep him away from the football field.* Is he as deaf and blind as his mother was when she was still technically alive but was less aware of her surroundings than a clam? Granted, they said test score averages in Flora had never been higher and had been climbing for five years, up to 87.59, more than two points above East High, which had a much bigger budget. Average absences, in the other direction, had plummeted to 3.3 per student per year, the lowest in eastern Colorado. Juvenile crime, drug use, smoking, premarital pregnancy, and alcohol use were all down. That was all well and good, but what did those things have to do with *him*? Or with Beethoven, for that matter? They came together every Saturday and played music. That's what kept them out of trouble, Stolz thought. The activity. Not him. Not Beethoven. If, instead of Beethoven, it was John Phillip Sousa or George M. Cohan or Henry Mancini, would the results have been any different?

His coffee has become cold and bitter. Stolz pours the remaining three-quarters of it down the kitchen sink, rinses out the mug, dries it, and hangs it on the wooden hook affixed to a wooden red-red-robin nailed to the wall. It had been a Valentine's Day gift when he was a child. From his mother.

> *"Wake up, wake up you sleepy head,*
> *Get up, get out of your bed,*
> *Cheer up, cheer up the sun is red,*
> *Live, love, laugh and be happy."*

Stolz returns upstairs and showers, but is unable to scrub off his doubts, which cling to him like pine tar. He dries himself, ties his flannel robe tightly around his expanding waist, and returns to the bedroom to ask Ann Smith if she wants Cheerios or Shredded Wheat (the large biscuit kind, which he prefers) for breakfast. He cracks opened the door and peers into the gloom to see if she is awake. She must be, because she is gone.

In his mentally disheveled state, Stolz assumes the worst. She has left him. Why? Or more likely, why not? For five years she has done everything for him he asked, to the point where she seemed to know what he wanted before he even asked, and what had she asked for in return? Nothing. She has never asked for anything. Nor has he ever given her anything. She has been his librarian, secretary, communications director, publicity director, house cleaner, cheerleader, mental therapist, and finally, willing bed partner, though he was never sure whether she, or he, enjoyed that part. Willing was true, though. He would never have tried to force her, or seduce her, even if he knew how.

The first time was a year-and-a-half ago, the same day he had buried his mother. A cold November morning, the kind of morning where his mother would cheerily proclaim, "The frost is on the pumpkin," when she still had the ability to talk. When she would have made him Cream of Wheat with Log Cabin syrup for breakfast and pulled on his hat with flaps until it was on good and tight, and clip his mittens with fleece lining to the cuffs of his coat before sending him off to school. Even though her mind had died long before, her body had died in the right season, a withered autumn oak leaf, brittle and brown, that fell silently off the tree without even a breath of a breeze and, upon contact with the earth, disintegrated.

After the burial, Ann Smith offered to drive Stolz home. He didn't refuse. They sat in his living room, she in a black dress, he in a characterless black suit he had bought for the funeral at the wholesale men's clothing outlet. As she often did, she waited for Stolz to be the first to say something. But he had nothing to say and just sat, looking not at her but out the window, pretending to be interested in passing cars. Finally, she said, "Would you like me to undress, Mr. Stolz?" He nodded. "Yes. I suppose."

They went upstairs, she to his bedroom and he into the bathroom to disrobe. He returned when the lights were out and the shades drawn. She was under a blanket. He lay next to her and probed her flesh timidly, finding her abdominal muscles to be surprisingly taut, and then rolled on top of her. They did it, wordlessly, finding and feeling each other with closed eyes since it wasn't yet dark enough for them not to be able to see each other's nakedness. Stolz wondered, but couldn't tell, whether or not she was a virgin, as he had no previous experience to compare it to. He placed a hand around her throat, gently at first, and she complied without resistance, her arms at her sides. After they were done, they took showers, one at a time, and dressed. Ann Smith put her glasses back on and her hair back in a bun, washed the soiled sheets in the washing machine, and remade the bed. They ate canned beef stew for dinner and, when it was late, went to bed together, to sleep. They didn't talk about it. Having sex seemed not to have altered their relationship, at least as far as Stolz could tell, which had been his greatest fear.

And now she's gone. A vague but all-encompassing emptiness overcomes Stolz, fleetingly sensing what his deaf and blind mother must have felt every moment of her final years. It makes him dizzy, just as it had on the podium in front of the orchestra five years before. He has to sit down on the edge of the bed or he will fall. He closes his eyes and puts his head in his hands. Where can she have gone? Should he search for her? If she has truly left him, that must mean she didn't want to be here, so what good would it do to look for her? If she doesn't want to come back, then he might not even want her to. And what right did he have to...?

He closes his eyes and lies down on his side. Five years. The Sequence has been completed. It could go on and on. Theoretically. There were always four orchestras in the pipeline, the fifth to squirt out like toothpaste from a tube, in September. Or it could stop. Let someone else do it. He has spawned five orchestras' worth of children who are now scattered out in the world somewhere. What are they doing? Who knows? Maybe some of them still play their instruments. Probably most of them have already forgotten who he is. Or maybe, "Yeah, that Beethoven stuff was okay, but that Mr. Stolz, he was a weird dude." He can't even remember most of their names. It was like one of those wildlife documentaries he would occasionally watch on TV, where the shrimp or some strange-looking fish would shoot out thousands of eggs into the water and then they would swim away. It was over. One out of a thousand, or some such ridiculously low percentage, would survive to adulthood. No, he would go back to the comfortable anonymity of the welder, and if after a time, that became unbearable—

"Layton!"

Stolz opens his eyes. It's Ann.

"Layton, are you upstairs?"

He pretends she has awakened him. That all is normal.

"Yes, I'm here."

"I just went out and got the *Ledger*. I wanted to be the first one. I got two copies. I think you'll like the headline."

"Okay. I'll be right down."

"Do you want Cheerios or Shredded Wheat?"

Ann Smith never takes credit for any of Layton Stolz's achievements. On this occasion though, she takes reflected pride to be the one to read the writeup in the *Flora Daily Ledger*.

"'*Stolz and Beethoven Shut Up Feds!*'"

"Feds?" Stolz asks. "What feds?"

"Let's see, shall we? '*On a memorable night in Flora, liberty struck a harmonious blow against tyranny.*'"

Stolz listens, astounded, at the description of the competing assemblies. He had been so preoccupied with preparing for the concert that he had no idea what was going on elsewhere. Town Hall? Phillip Valentine? The column went on to list all of Flora's academic achievements since the inception of the Beethoven Sequence.

"Who wrote the article?"

"A Sandy Duckworthy. Junior staff writer."

"What did he say about the music?" Stolz asks.

"He's a she, I think."

"Doesn't she say anything about the music?"

"I'm just getting to that," Ann Smith says. "Just hold your horses." She says that last part with a smile and a wink to make sure Stolz knows it is a jest, since they occur so rarely.

"'*This reporter has seldom heard a concert as inspiring by anyone, anywhere.*' That's nice. I'll write her a thank you note—"

"And send her flowers," Stolz adds. His mother liked flowers.

"But how's that for a glowing review?"

Before he can answer, the phone rings.

"Mr. Stolz? Mr. Layton Stolz? Arlene Covington speaking. You don't know me. I'm calling from Dubuque. Dubuque, Iowa. I'm the director of music in the public schools out here and I just read in the *Telegraph Herald* about your remarkable performance last night."

"*Telegraph Herald*? What were they doing out here?" Stolz asks.

Arlene Covington lets out a big city chuckle.

"They weren't out there, Mr. Stolz. It's that the AP picked up the *Daily Ledger* story on the wires and ran with it. I imagine '*Stolz and Beethoven Shut Up Feds!*' is in just about every major city daily this morning."

Stolz isn't sure how he is supposed to respond, so he doesn't say anything.

"Mr. Stolz," Covington continues. "You must be a busy man and I don't want to waste your time, so I'll get to the point. We want you to come out here to Dubuque to start a Beethoven Sequence, just like you did in Flora."

"Hold on," Stolz says. He covers the receiver with his hand and lips Covington's message to Ann Smith. He shrugs, a silent request for her advice. She, in turn, whispers the words he should say back.

"Miss Covington," Stolz says.

"Mrs."

"Mrs. Covington, thank you for your interest. But I have a full time job here in Flora."

Covington assures him that he would be paid for his time, and given that it is almost summer vacation for the schools, he could schedule some time to come to Dubuque at his convenience over the next three months. Before Stolz can ask any follow-up questions, Covington informs him that, in addition to being director of music in the Dubuque public schools, she is also vice president of the National School Music Educators Association. And that if things work out well in Dubuque, as she fully expects them to, there is no telling how many Beethoven Sequences could be established across the entire country.

Layton Stolz then has another of his moments of inspired intuition.

"Mrs. Covington," he says. "I appreciate your generosity. But before I agree to anything, there's one thing I would have to insist on."

"And what would that be?" The tone of Covington's voice suggests she had offered all she is going to offer, like a car dealer—"Let me speak to my manager"—before sealing the deal.

"Everyone I train has to agree to follow my instructions exactly," Stolz says. "To the letter. And everyone who that person might train as well. Otherwise, the program will end up...different."

Covington sounds relieved. This won't cost her anything.

"I don't think that will be a problem," she says. "We have a deal, then?"

Ann Smith, who has been listening, nodded affirmatively.

"Yes. Yes, we have a deal," Stolz says.

Covington chuckles again.

"What are you laughing at?" Stolz asks. He doesn't like being laughed at, which Covington seems to sense.

"Oh, sorry. Don't mind me. Just that you sure put that DC bigwig, Valentine, in his place!"

Chapter Seven

Even after Stolz accepts Arlene Covington's offer, he still does not anticipate many takers, if at all, given the stringent requirement he has insisted upon. But he is wrong. Word has gotten around. At first unbeknownst to him, his former students by the hundreds had become missionaries of a sort, buttonholing any music educators they could corral to tell them about the Beethoven Sequence experience. As he learns, little by little, how they have extended his program's notoriety, Stolz hopes they didn't exaggerate the successes simply to aggrandize themselves. But after a few months, so many school music teachers flock to his doorstep, it soon reaches the point where he can't handle the workload alone and still conduct his own orchestras.

It is then he has another brainstorm. He invites his best former students, some of whom are already graduating college, to live in his house with him, expense free. His home becomes a mini-conservatory where, with a month of intense training, he teaches them how to train other Beethoven Sequence teachers. They become his disciples, more grateful and more devoted than ever. Duane Sheely, the violist who is a graduate of the original Sequence class in Flora, is one. Ballard Whitmore, the young Mormon boy, is not. What has happened to him, on or after his mission, is unknown to Stolz, leaving him with an indefinable emptiness. Maybe he should have talked to the boy's parents and convinced them to allow Ballard to continue with his music and forego the mission. But that is all in the past. So many others do come back, and now, rather than having an endless stream of wannabes come to Flora for Stolz to train, his own handpicked apostles spread the

Gospel according to Layton Stolz far and wide across the country.

It has been difficult enough for Stolz to lead a double life as a machine shop worker and a maestro. But now, to add that third career as a music educator, it is no longer feasible for him to do it all. He has no doubt of his mission in life, but the problem is that he doesn't know if he can earn a living as a musician. Conducting has been his passion, and when he started he had no concept of what the future might have in store. Yes, the arrangement with Arlene Covington has worked out conveniently. But that was a one-shot deal, and the money he had saved from it has been all but eaten up by the food and lodging he offered his students, from whom he refused any compensation. The conducting he did at Flora and most of the training he had provided had also been offered gratis. If he had dared charge money, or if at some point someone had said "no thanks, we can live without your orchestra and your ideas," his ambitions could have quickly been stopped dead in their tracks. Being a welder might not satisfy his creative urge, but at least he could depend on a paycheck every other week. It paid his expenses—his mortgage, his auto payments, his food. Modest expenses, but expenses nevertheless. Something had to give.

"Let me take care of it," Ann Smith says. "Let me do some research at the library."

Within a month, the Beethoven Sequence Association, condensed into the acronym BSA, was formed as a charitable, 501(c)(3) organization, with a handpicked board of faithful trustees, a staff comprising Ann Smith, Duane Sheely, three volunteers, and a local CPA who donated his services as an in-kind contribution. At their first meeting, the board pledged over a million dollars. Layton Stolz was given a blank check to continue to perform his magic. The next day, he handed in his two-weeks' notice to the Johnson Machine Shop. His workmates offered to give him a going away party, but he declined.

Within two years, the phenomenon of the Sequence swept across the country like a Rocky Mountain gale. Stolz is labeled a genius and the "Pied Piper of classical music." He is interviewed on Terri Gross's Fresh Air radio show and is a lead segment on 60 Minutes with Mike Wallace. Throughout it all he keeps a viselike grip on his acolytes, not permitting them to stray one iota from their training. For all five years of the Sequence, everything emanates from Layton Stolz, passes through his disciples, and works its way down to the individual conductors. Every musical phrase, every hand gesture is taught and practiced and practiced over again. Yet, rather than bristle against such taut supervision, the acolytes, most of whom came from humble artistic beginnings, are uniformly radiant. They know they are special, and they're on a mission for which success is all but guaranteed. Those few conductors who wander from the straight and narrow are summarily relieved of their duties. Not a word of reprimand needs to be issued because the humiliation of expulsion, followed by complete ostracization, is more punishment than most aspiring conductors can bear or afford.

The town of Smirewood in Allamakee County, Iowa, an unobtrusive agricultural community surrounded by amber waves of grain, proudly embraced the Sequence program. Young Duane Sheely has been the Smirewood High School orchestra conductor for a year and was instrumental in initiating its chapter membership. As if touched by a saint, Sheely's complexion has cleared miraculously as he transitioned from adolescence into manhood, his hair has degreased and is now trim and well-maintained, and he hasn't smoked a cigarette since the day Stolz told him to quit. He imposes similarly stringent restrictions on his own students, and they respond accordingly: No drugs, no alcohol, no long hair, no messy clothes. No premarital sex. Students can ill afford to stray. If they don't abide, they're out of the program—there is always someone waiting in the wings, clamoring to get in. Everyone knows what's at stake.

There is one other behavior Sheely will not tolerate, with which he deals even more severely than the others. Bullying. If he sees one student belittling another, regardless of how talented that student is, he or she is out. That is no doubt the product of his memories of the pummeling he had received at the hardened fists of the Fightin' Bisons offensive line, which had left him bruised, humiliated, and helpless. The taunting—pizza face, queer, and faggot—were as hurtful as the thrashings. More hurtful. Outnumbered and outmuscled, Sheely's only recourse had been to accept getting his ass kicked on a regular basis. Until the Sequence. Layton Stolz had literally been his savior.

The abuse Sheely endured accounts for his antipathy to bullying of any sort, starting from school and extending to broader society. So even though he is sympathetic to the message of freedom and brotherhood in Beethoven's music, it is the message of liberation that resonates with him to his core. No one—neither individuals nor governments—should have the right to force anyone else to do something. If government is oppressive, the people have the right to resist.

Sheely's tenure at Smirewood coincided with the traveling three-ring circus that came through Iowa every four years, also known as the Iowa caucuses. The speeches, the photo ops at local diners, the visits to the Grange hall. "I'll protect the farmers!" "I'll raise your subsidies!" "I'll cut your taxes!" "I'll get you better paying jobs!" "I'll save small business!" "I've got a plan!" If you took the Republican or Democrat labels off their nametags, Sheely thought, for the most part you couldn't tell one from the other. He pretty much ignored them all. It really didn't matter who was nominated or even who was elected president. They all went through the same sausage maker in DC, and in the end all sausages taste pretty much the same. The only difference is how much gristle gets stuck in your teeth.

One presidential candidate Sheely did not ignore was U.S. Representative Sheffield Harrington from Massachusetts—"folks call me Sheff"—the ranking member of the House Oversight Committee. Harrington had been a fixture in Congress for two decades and an icon in Massachusetts politics even longer, beginning when he was a fresh-faced attorney and waged a one-man war on the corruption in the State House. Though the results of his crusade were Pyrrhic—he lost his first campaign for state office, and corruption was as rampant as ever—the effort endeared him to the voters, which paid off in the long run. Harrington also had the personal touch. A scion of the wealth and privilege of a Boston family that went back to the Mayflower, he was at the same time a man of the people. His constituents loved him for showing up unannounced to shop at rural general stores, wearing down-to-earth New England flannels, to sample apple cider doughnuts in the autumn. Or when he'd take less fortunate youths, both boys and girls, on fishing excursions off Nantucket in his Carver C52 Outboard Yacht. He had a reputation as a backroom wheeler-dealer who got things done, but now, as far as Sheely was concerned, he was using Iowans as props while promising things, like giving unlimited handouts to people who were too lazy to work, shutting down coal mines and restricting fracking, and giving free education and health care to people who came into the country illegally. It wasn't so much that Sheely was against these things in principle—of course he didn't want people to starve or be sick—as how it was all going to be paid for. Harrington was the odds-on favorite to win not only the caucus, but also the nomination, and perhaps even the general election. He was a master sweet-talker, but, once you sifted out all the sugar, the answer was clear. As much as Sheff hemmed and hawed, he couldn't deny the reality of his platform: The hardworking taxpayer was going to be forced to pay for it. Through the teeth. To Sheely's way of thinking, that was governmental bullying at its worst, and it was intolerable.

Harrington arrived in Smirewood on the back leg of his second Iowa campaign swing to give a speech. The caucus is three days away. The Saturday morning event, to be held on the stage of the Smirewood High School auditorium, is billed as a major policy address, but everyone knows in advance what it's going to be about, since all the candidates have laid out their turf for so long and so often that it has gone to seed. Sheely does not want to see his fellow townspeople and—with sound bites of the speech reverberating on all the news outlets—the rest of the nation suckered by Harrington's spit-polished rhetoric. He also grouses that his Saturday morning Beethoven rehearsal space is being preempted by a politician, regardless of his stripe.

Recalling the giddy evening two years before when Phillip Valentine was ridden out of Flora on a rail, Sheely decides to emulate his mentor and idol, Layton Stolz. Sheely has been in Smirewood for less than two years, so performing the Ninth Symphony to drown out the political cock-and-bull stories is not in the cards, as it is still more than three years away. He comes up with an alternate plan, and makes a phone call to nearby Dubuque and speaks to Arlene Covington, who had given Stolz his big start. Maybe she could help again. Sheely shares his idea.

On Saturday morning, while Sheff is introduced and extoled inside the school, gathering outside is a colossal orchestra of almost two hundred students, comprising almost every student in Iowa who is or had been a participant of the Sequence. When Sheff begins his speech—"Folks, there's nothing prettier than a sunny morning in Smirewood"—Sheely and Covington silently march their troops into opposite wings of the auditorium stage. When Sheff declares, "The people of Iowa deserve to know what each of us candidates stands for. Let me be clear—" the orchestra is in position. When Sheff says, "Here is my plan," that is the cue.

Sheely and Covington simultaneously give a vigorous downbeat of the rousing coda of Beethoven's *Egmont Overture*, having instructed the students to play as loudly as they can. As on the previous occasion, the din drowns out everything the speaker says. Only the cheers of the people defending individual liberty can be heard above it. Harrington stands open-mouthed at the podium, dumbfounded, until one of his aides approaches and tells him to keep smiling while they try to quell the insurrection. So he does, looking no less a dummy than Charlie McCarthy, which is not to his political advantage, especially as the cameras continue shooting his photo, which will be seen around the world on the evening's news.

In the meantime, Harrington's security contingent rushes to the wings and demands that the combined orchestras cease and desist immediately. Sheely and Covington continue conducting. The orchestras continue playing, putting the security people in a real quandary. They could start arresting students, hauling them off as they cling to their instruments, which would enable Harrington to resume his speech. But how would it look to the rest of the world—for the rest of the world would surely see it—for them to be dragging two-hundred well-dressed, well-behaved, over-achieving Iowa classical music students? They quickly decide it wouldn't look good. The band plays on.

Afterwards, Sheely and Covington meet at the malt shop across the street from the high school, toasting each other's success over a chocolate milkshake. Silver-haired Arlene Covington, a wearer of sensible shoes and two generations senior to Sheely, says, "That's the most fun I've had in years! I never thought being a music teacher I'd ever get close to being arrested!"

Duane Sheely smiles back. They click glasses so energetically that they each spill a little of their shake, but they don't care. Sheely is thinking, it might have been fun for her, but what they had just accomplished was more than fun for him. Once again the power of music had been a bulwark against government overreach. Sequence equals power. Power equals Sequence.

The votes are in. Harrington runs a weak fourth in the caucus. Five days later, his poll numbers having plummeted, Sheffield Harrington drops out of the race. "If he can't lick a high school orchestra, how can he lick Phillip Valentine?" is the rallying cry. What Harrington does lick are his wounds, and resigns himself to running for reelection for his House seat, with an all-but-guaranteed outcome, after which he would successfully maneuver his way to becoming Speaker and the most powerful legislator in the land. In the meantime, Duane Sheely, who has overnight become a local celebrity, is asked by a reporter from the *Allamakee Intelligencer* the source of his inspiration to "slam a Beethoven," coining a phrase that would soon catch on nationwide. His response is, "I owe it all to Layton Stolz." Sandy Duckworthy, the reporter who covered the original "Beethoven slamming" for the *Flora Daily Ledger*, read the *Intelligencer* article with interest and filed it under Stolz, Layton. She has a hunch it will be a story to continue following.

The Smirewood protest lit a match in a highly inflammable, bone-dry political forest. In a single day, the Sequence had been transformed from a music program into a political weapon with the lethal accuracy of a Patriot guided missile. Anytime Big Government threatened, "slamming a Beethoven" was there to subdue it. Speakers had to make a difficult calculation: Keep the venue of their events secret, changing them at the last minute if necessary, or contour their positions to be more amenable to the local gentry's bias toward smaller government. For "the little people," the effect was empowering because a potent countermeasure to effectively combat the contagion of big business, big money, and big government, which had increasingly been infecting their political landscape, had miraculously materialized. There were some who were uncomfortable with, or even distressed by, tactics that could easily be described as heavy-handed and intimidating. But even they, too, acquiesced, because the Sequence was so popular, the music was so great, the things it had done for education and for building model citizens were so wonderful. And, after all, it was all about freedom. Who could argue with that?

Chapter Eight

There are one-hundred-forty-three Beethoven Sequence chapters throughout the country. Every chapter's hierarchical organizational structure is the same, consisting of a chair, treasurer, and secretary, with a group of dedicated volunteers at its beck and call to serve the needs of the student musicians. There is nothing mysterious about the structure. It's absolutely cookie-cutter. The only thing unusual about it is that directions for a chapter's activities are handed down by Layton Stolz through his minions. The individual chapter has only to follow instructions to be rewarded. Not following instructions is not an option.

In the nation's heartland, where school orchestra programs had never been as entrenched as band and choir, the Sequence program fills a vacuum and is wildly popular. On the coasts, competing against well-established programs is a more formidable challenge, but even there the Sequence is gaining a serious toehold, especially in school districts on the lower rungs of the economic ladder. The reason is simple. The Sequence produces dramatic, quantifiable results and costs the schools nothing. Further, institutions of post-high school education, from trade schools to private universities, have only to see which school districts had instituted the Sequence to determine which students would be strong candidates for admission. Playing in a Sequence orchestra is almost a guarantee to a college scholarship.

Though it has been several years since Layton Stolz curtailed his hands-on conducting, literally passing the baton to his disciples, he remains the BSA's glowing, molten core. White hot, like the acetylene torch he once wielded, Stolz is the organization's throbbing brain, its nerve center.

At his prompting, the BSA created an annual two-week Beethoven Institute, held every June in a different city. At the Institute, Stolz invited the world's most eminent Beethoven scholars—historians, musicologists, and theorists—to give lectures and presentations about the great composer's life and music. Stolz himself held daily Institute workshops devoted to one-on-one Sequence training with new disciples. In addition to the annual national Institute, there are monthly regional conferences throughout the year that Stolz attends religiously, where he receives up-to-the-minute feedback from his eight regional directors and coordinates their activities. The regional directors, in turn, spread the gospel to state directors whose responsibility it then is to make sure the local chapters receive the resources they need to keep the program as pure and focused as Layton Stolz's initial vision. The public is welcome to attend any of the activities of the national Institute and regional conferences at no cost, though they do have to pay for meals and lodging. At the conferences, visitors can soak up all the new scholarship there is to be had about Beethoven, find out what wonderful things are being accomplished by Sequence students around the country, and hobnob with guest artist, lecturers, and the entire hierarchy of the BSA organization.

To oversee the effective implementation of Layton Stolz's vision, the BSA leased three floors of a new glass and steel office building in Denver's Tech Center, about ten miles south of downtown. From those premises, the organization controls its swelling undertakings. It was assumed Stolz would take the most grandiose space on the third floor, a corner office with a sweeping view of the Rockies. Instead, not wanting to waste time climbing stairs or waiting for an elevator, Stolz chose a modest room on the first floor, which had the attraction of an enclosed outside patio area, with a little greenery and a picnic table. It wasn't rural Flora, but it helped him feel more at home. Though when he thinks about it, which isn't often, he doesn't miss Flora at all. Flora is a place where he had once lived and worked, but the people there, he came to realize, were no different than the people anywhere else. No better, no worse. To Stolz, the only important thing was *what* he was doing, not where.

Having the first floor office also makes it convenient for his daily meeting with his staff, which takes place for precisely one hour, upon their entering the building at eight a.m.. From nine to ten, Stolz receives phone calls from anyone with questions for him: conductors, regional directors, alumni, even students. From ten to eleven is media hour, during which he conducts interviews either face to face, which is his preference, or by phone if not. That particular time slot was chosen so that it would not be too early on the west coast nor too late on the east for such communications. Overseas interviews are given no special consideration. Sometimes his interviews are live, others are taped for later broadcast. Some people in the public spotlight prefer the latter format because the interviews can be edited for audio blemishes, which, like photoshopping the acne off of students' high school yearbook photos, sanitizes the end product. But Stolz doesn't care one way or the other. His message is simple, it has never changed, and he has been saying it for years.

From eleven to noon, Ann Smith informs him of any developments she thinks should be brought to his attention, discusses planning for upcoming conferences, and delivers the mail sent to the BSA that morning, placing the pile in a wooden box on the upper right hand corner of his desk. When he has time, Stolz takes a cursory look at them in order to start considering an appropriate response. Later in the afternoon, when the day's business is over, he answers each inquiry with a handwritten letter. Ann Smith suggested doing that every day would exhaust him, but Stolz, pointing to the framed rejection letter from Juilliard that occupied a prominent place on his office desk between the mailbox and the photo of his mother, insisted on keeping up the practice year after year. From noon to one, Stolz has lunch, usually a bologna sandwich on white bread, sometimes with mustard, sometimes without, sometimes in his office, sometimes on the patio. From one o'clock until two is the hour Stolz savors. It is the hour during which he studies the music and life of Beethoven, brooking no intrusion. If the weather is fair, he does his studying on his little patio as well.

From two to three Stolz is updated on BSA's promotional activities. It isn't something he is particularly interested in, but he understands the necessity. BSA Central sends out a monthly e-newsletter to hundreds of thousands of people, updating them on all the organization's most recent successes. BSA's social media staff comprises young people who constantly post videos of various student orchestras' performances from around the country, links to the almost daily news articles about the program's achievements, updates on graduating students receiving scholarships to the most prestigious universities, and the like. At Stolz's personal directive, the media staff is instructed to shy away from the increasing popularity and number of "Beethoven slammings." If local and national media want to cover those stories, that is their business, but Stolz insists that he and the BSA remain politically neutral.

Additional staff are liaisons with the traditional media, in regular contact with major national and local newspapers, and television and radio stations. The only proviso is that information sent to any and every media contact, social or traditional, has to first be approved by BSA Central. No one, either on a local, state, or regional level, is permitted to post a photo, issue a statement, or even promote a concert, without first sending it up the ladder. "We don't want to muddy the waters with a mixed message," is the very clear message handed down by Layton Stolz. And since the organization is functioning so efficiently, it is never a problem. Permission usually takes but a few minutes and is rarely denied.

From three to four, Stolz meets with his CFO to talk about budget and fundraising opportunities. The beauty of BSA's financial model is that no one in the organization, all the way down to a first-year Sequence student, has to pay for anything. No student has to pay for an instrument, ever. No school has to pay for music, ever. No concertgoer has to pay for a ticket to a Beethoven Sequence performance, ever. The BSA administration, the leased office space, the regional meetings, and the Institute, all of that is paid for. How? Not by the government. Stolz refused to accept a cent of public money. People work hard to make a living. Why should their taxes go to a private organization when it's difficult as it is to buy a house and raise a family? No, all BSA's funding comes from charitable giving: corporations, philanthropic organizations, individuals, alumni. How do they manage? Because of the music of Beethoven. And because of the success. Those are the two key, essential elements. So, whenever the CFO suggests some new angle to raise money that diverges from their core values, Stolz immediately quashes it.

At four o'clock, Stolz typically returns to the letters that Ann Smith has left in his mailbox. He always answers the ones from students first. Thank-you notes to six-figure donors can wait until last. Today, there is a letter from a tenth-grade girl from Blytheville, Arkansas, who wants to let him know she's learning to make her own oboe reeds. God bless her, Stolz thinks. Should he tell her that if she wants to be a professional oboist she is going to spend half the rest of her life making reeds? He decides not to mention that. Instead, he congratulates her on her accomplishment and tells her he is certain making her own reeds will help her play the cadenza in the first movement of the Fifth Symphony even more beautifully.

Then there is the letter from the alumnus who just got his teaching certification. He wants to move to Newark, New Jersey from his home Bozeman, Montana, to begin an inner-city Sequence program for poor people of color. What should he do to get started? Stolz congratulates him, too, both for getting his certification and for having such noble intentions. He provides the contact information to the appropriate staffer in charge of start-ups. "Make sure this young man gets all the resources he needs," he writes at the bottom.

And so on. No letter he writes is under a page long. There is a good reason for that. In his whole life, he had received one letter from his father, which he memorized, verbatim, in its entirety. It was on the reverse side of a postcard of a grizzly bear, which his father sent him when he and his drinking buddies went on a guys' road trip to Yellowstone National Park, leaving his mother and him at home. The letter read: "Hey Lonny, what do you think of the size of this sucker, huh? Your Dad."

Chapter Nine

"Mind if we brush on a little color, Dr. Stolz?"

"What do you mean? And I'm not a doctor. It's mister."

"Studio lights. Make everyone look pasty as a cadaver. This'll just make you look nice and healthy."

"Okay. Go ahead."

Out comes a brush. Stolz closes his eyes so the powdery makeup won't get in them.

"Trim those eyebrows for you?"

"No."

"Dr. Stolz," comes another voice, "I'm just going to run this wire up through your shirt. Can you pull it out above your top button?"

"Okay. Then what do I do?"

"I'll take care of that. I'm just going to clip it on to your collar. How is that?"

"Fine. Do I have to talk into it?"

"No. Just speak normally. We'll take care of the rest."

"Ten seconds! Smile at the host, Dr. Stolz. Five. Okay, we're on."

"Welcome to *Good Morning, America*," the host, Diane Sawyer, says into the camera swinging in her direction. "We've got a very special guest in our studio this morning. Layton Stolz, the creator of the phenomenon, the Beethoven Sequence, that's sweeping the country. Classical music. Go figure! And joining him are eight more very special guests: students from Westbury High School on Long Island, New York.

"Mr. Stolz, how long have you known these young men and women?"

"About five minutes. I met them backstage, just before we went on."

"So you had no time to prep them on their answers?"

Chuckling from all except Stolz.

"No."

"Okay, kids. Tell us about your experience with the Beethoven Sequence."

The students from Westbury High have been selected for the show for two reasons. The school has a diverse mix of races, religions, and ethnic backgrounds, many of which are represented by the students in the studio. The second reason is that in the four years since the school instituted the Sequence—their first Ninth Symphony is slated for the coming spring—Westbury High realized the most dramatic improvements in test scores, attendance, and dropout rates of any school in the country.

The eight students speak effusively and eloquently about all the great things that have been accomplished in the past four years with their orchestra conductor, Mr. Lewis, who has followed Layton Stolz's program to the letter. The discipline, the teamwork, the hours of study and practice, all have made them better students.

"Hats off to you, students. And that seems to be what's happening all around America these days," Sawyer says. "What do you say to that, Mr. Stolz?"

"Well, I'm very happy to hear about all those good results."

"I'm glad you think so."

More good-natured laughing.

"But," Stolz continues, "that's not the reason I started the Sequence."

"No? Do tell."

"I started it because the music of Beethoven is inspirational in itself. The music, itself, makes people want to be better people. And the particular compositions I chose of his reflect America's values of freedom and liberty. I guess you can say it touches our revolutionary spirit."

"Well put, Mr. Stolz. Well put. Before we break, I just want to ask you about a recent news story. I'm sure you heard about it."

"What's that?"

"Out in Salt Lake City, a young high school orchestra conductor named, let's see, Ballard Whitmore, says he has made some adjustments to the Sequence. He said he didn't see why it was necessary to perform those specific songs by Beethoven, or even anything at all by Beethoven, for that matter. He said, and I quote, 'While I admire the amazing accomplishments Layton Stolz has made for music and for education, there's room for flexibility within his system. Since every student has his own strengths and areas where she or he can improve, I try to address the needs of each student as an individual.' Mr. Whitmore claims to have gotten equally positive results from his students over the past three years, and the test scores his school provided seem to bear that out."

Stolz keeps his eyes on Sawyer, but says nothing. Dead air time is the worst no-no on television.

"Mr. Stolz?" Sawyer asks. "Any comment about Whitmore's claims? Are you contemplating broadening the Sequence program?"

They had all recited *'Twas the Night Before Christmas* together. Now it was the night after Christmas and not a creature is stirring, except little Layton. His parents are sleeping downstairs in Aunt Irma and Uncle Cy's guestroom. Layton was given his own "special" room upstairs, which he knows is not really a bedroom at all, but his uncle's office in which they put a cot for their stay.

Without turning on the light, Layton leaves the room with one of his new lollipop-decorated pillows and tiptoes down the hallway and past the bathroom. He silently opens the door to his aunt and uncle's bedroom. They lay sleeping, each in their own twin bed. It had been a long, exciting day, ending with a huge meal in which everyone ate too much turkey and ham and apple pie. The adults had drunk some wine. Everyone was tired, and his aunt and uncle are sleeping soundly. At least, his uncle is, judging from the volume of his snoring.

Layton stands quietly until his eyes adjust to the darkness. When he is able to see his Aunt Irma's outline, he approaches the side of her bed, and without hesitation covers her head with his new hypoallergenic pillow. At first she doesn't move, but then when she realizes she is having difficulty breathing, she reaches for the pillow. Layton presses down harder with all his body weight, smothering Aunt Irma's attempt to call out for help as she struggles and thrashes about. Uncle Cy continues to snore.

Layton hasn't counted on Aunt Irma being stronger than he is. When it becomes clear he can't hold her down any longer and his plan will not succeed, he relents and removes the pillow.

Aunt Irma is panting.

"My God, Layton," she whispers, "what in heavens did you think you were doing?"

"I was scared in my room," he says. "I just wanted to sleep next to you. I didn't realize…"

He holds out his new pillow.

"See?" he says. "I brought it."

Aunt Irma can't see Layton's face in the dark. She thinks for a moment before responding.

"Well, okay," she says. "But you certainly gave me a fright. Now come lie down next to me, and we won't say another word about it."

"Mr. Stolz?" Sawyer asks.

"What?

"Mr. Whitmore's claims?"

"It's a free country," Stolz says.

"It is, indeed. Thank you, Layton Stolz and students from Westbury High. We're rooting for you. We'll be back after this commercial break to show you how to make perfect pesto in ten minutes."

They pull his microphone down through his shirt and give him a cloth to wipe off his makeup. Ann Smith is waiting in the wings.

"Don't worry," she says. "I'll take care of it."

"I hadn't heard about this. Why didn't anyone tell me?"

"It's a small story."

"But it's that boy. The one who went on a mission. He was such a good boy. What happened? What is he doing?"

"Don't worry," Ann Smith repeats. "He's an unknown out to be a big frog in a small pond."

"That's not the point."

"As I said, I'll take care of it. You needn't worry."

"I do worry. Set up a call for me with him."

"All right."

Layton Stolz returns to his hotel room. He has three hours before he has to leave for the airport to return home. He had planned to study Thayer's biography of Beethoven, his bible, but is too agitated. He roams his room like a caged cat in a zoo. He fills a plastic cup of water from the bathroom sink but neglects to drink it. He attempts, unsuccessfully, to open the room's windows. He rolls his suitcase, already packed, to the door, three feet from where it had been next to the dresser. He opens the minifridge to inspect its contents and just as he decides to splurge for a KitKat, the room phone rings.

"I've got Mr. Whitmore on the line," Ann Smith says.

"Put him on."

Stolz waits.

"Mr. Stolz?" It's Whitmore.

"Ballard," Stolz says. "So good to hear your voice. It has been a long time."

"I agree," Whitmore said. "Too long! I'm sorry I haven't stayed in touch."

"No problem, Ballard. No problem. Tell me, what have you been up to?"

"Well, there's not all that much to tell. After high school I went on a mission to Sao Paolo—"

"Sao Paolo! That's pretty exotic, isn't it?"

Whitmore laughs.

"Oh, not really. The church has a big presence down there. And as you might know, we have pretty strict rules for what we're allowed to do. But you'll be happy to know they let me play my violin! I couldn't practice every day or anything like that but at least I got to play once in a while, and even played some Beethoven sonatas with a pianist down there. I thought of you."

"That's a good boy. So in a way, you were almost a missionary for Beethoven, too."

"Yes, I guess you could say that."

"And what have you been doing since you got back?"

"Well, in a nutshell, I'm a grad student at BYU. And, I'm married!"

"Married! Well, congratulations! Another musician?"

"No, she's a business major. She's too smart to be a musician."

Whitmore must have realized he probably shouldn't have said that because he is suddenly silent.

"That's okay, Ballard. I know exactly what you mean," Stolz says. "But I read in the paper that you were conducting a high school orchestra. Is that true?"

"Don't always believe what you read, Mr. Stolz."

"So you're not doing that?" Stolz is relieved. Maybe it had all been a mistake. Newspapers can be like that.

"Well, in a way, I guess I am. I had to do a graduate project for my masters, so I found a low-income high school on the west side that has a really small orchestra. Since the conductor also does the band and chorus, he was happy for me to help out. I'm volunteering, really. There are a lot of immigrant kids, like from South America and Polynesia, eastern Europe, southeast Asia, who have never heard classical music, so this is really new to them."

"That's a good thing you're doing," Stolz says. "And so you teach them the Sequence?"

"Mr. Stolz, I can't tell you how much I learned from you in Flora. It was so inspiring. I've tried to bring that same feeling to the school. I know that's impossible, but I think the kids are starting to catch on."

"You started with *Egmont?*"

"I'm sure I'll get to that at some point. But I thought it would be a good idea to start with some of their own traditional songs to get them excited, and then build up to Beethoven, so I wrote some arrangements for orchestra. That's what they're working on now."

"Some of these children—the ones from countries with despotic rulers—would no doubt benefit from Beethoven's message of freedom. Don't you think?"

"Absolutely. And as soon as they're ready, you can be sure we'll try to tackle it. That newspaper article. They didn't quote me entirely accurately. I'm sure you know what that's like."

"Certainly. Certainly. But that thing you said, that there's room for flexibility within the system…"

"Yes. I did say that. That part was correct."

"I see. And how is it that you and your bride manage, if you're only volunteering? How do you make ends meet?"

Whitmore laughed.

"We're living in the basement of her parents' house, that's how! Maybe when I graduate I'll get a real job."

Stolz doesn't need to hear any more.

"Well, good luck to you, Ballard."

The next day, and for the next two weeks, *The Salt Lake Tribune* and the other local daily, the *Deseret News*, owned by the Church of Jesus Christ of Latter-day Saints, more commonly known as the Mormon Church, receive letters to the editor extoling the virtues of the Beethoven Sequence and expressing veiled disapproval of Ballard Whitmore. With all the pressing issues of the day, when the first letter arrived, criticizing a BYU student who volunteers to teach music at a high school, the editors decided not to print it. But when a dozen arrived in their mailbox, they concluded it's in the public interest to publish a few of them. "If it ain't broke, don't fix it!" one wrote. "Last I heard, Layton Stolz knew what he was doing." "Ballard Whitmore is a good young man, but why he is trying to reinvent the wheel when it's been rolling smoothly?" "We need the Sequense [*sic*] for our children and grandchildren. How dare Ballard Whitmore take it from us!"

Layton Stolz does not want to hurt the boy, just send a subtle signal so that he'll return to the fold. Just so he understands how important it is to adhere to the program, for the boy's success as much as the Sequence's. And, in a roundabout way, to consider the consequences of straying.

Three weeks after the Diane Sawyer interview, Stolz is at his desk. It is eleven o'clock, time to skim through the daily mail. There are the usual gushing letters about how Beethoven has transformed lives, and some others with very specific questions about how to interpret and conduct certain passages. They are all quite routine, and Stolz can rattle off the appropriate responses in minutes—he has almost memorized the words by now.

"There's one from Duane Sheely," Ann Smith says.

"Let me guess," Stolz says. "Duane wants me to run for president."

"Yes, just as he asks you every month."

"Tell Duane when I win I'll make him vice president."

"He'll appreciate that."

"By now, he should realize I don't want to have anything to do with politics."

"So you say. But Duane's not the only one who wants you to run."

"Whatever."

Picking up the next letter, he notices the envelope has a Salt Lake City postmark. Opening it, he looks at it, and manages to not change his expression in front of Ann Smith. Typed on a plain piece of copy paper, in standard Times New Roman, 12-point, is one word, followed by a question mark. *Coriolan?* Signed by Ballard Whitmore. He places the letter face down on his desk.

"Is that it?" he asks.

"That's it," Ann Smith says.

"Thank you."

Ann Smith leaves his office. Stolz returns to the letter. He holds it the same way he had held the rejection letter from Juilliard, with trembling hands. The difference is, with Juilliard he did not know what the letter was going to say. With this one, he understands all too well what it means. He has not known such fear since his father returned home one night in a drunken stupor wielding a galvanized pipe from the machine shop. His mother and he locked themselves in the bathroom until Doug Stolz finished ranting, splintering their dining room furniture, and falling asleep on the kitchen floor.

Since Stolz doesn't smoke, he doesn't have a match or lighter to burn the letter. If he crumples it up in the waste paper basket it could be found by a janitor. He could cut it up with scissors and flush it down the toilet, but that could clog the drain and might cause people to wonder. He knows what he has to do. He tears the letter into little pieces, puts it inside his bologna sandwich, and eats it.

Chapter Ten

Two years later, at his morning meeting, it is with dismay that Layton Stolz receives troubling news from his protégé, Duane Sheely, newly appointed by Stolz as BSA Midwest Region director. Two years since his gentle dressing down, Ballard Whitmore's name is back in the public spotlight. He has given an interview on *Radio West*, the popular KUER-FM program broadcast from the University of Utah campus in Salt Lake City. Whitmore, having graduated BYU with honors, has had a fulltime job conducting the South High School orchestra and more recently was asked by the Salt Lake City government to lead an effort to develop a district-wide after-school music curriculum. Whitmore explained to the show's insightful host, Doug Fabrizio, why he felt compelled to make a clean break with the Beethoven Sequence, and how he has formulated his own locally based strategic plan for music education, which involves not only orchestra playing, but also singing, dancing, eurhythmics, and small ensemble training. Like Layton Stolz, Whitmore holds Saturday rehearsals. Unlike Stolz, he spends an additional two hours after school every day working one-on-one with elementary school children from low-income households, which has the added value of saving those students' parents some of the worry and expense of child care. Whitmore is now touting his program, All Together, as a viable option to the Sequence. What is particularly troubling for the BSA is that Whitmore's data-driven results are at least as promising as theirs.

Stolz is highly vexed about this development, though he tries to convince himself otherwise, because the BSA numbers have become staggering. There is a tightly-knit network of two-hundred-seventeen chapters of the

Beethoven Sequence spread across the country. Each chapter comprises five Sequence orchestras, and each orchestra has anywhere between thirty and seventy student musicians. Taking fifty as an average, this means at any given moment there are almost 55,000 students working diligently to learn to play Beethoven's music. Then add their supportive parents, another 100,000, more or less. Then add Sequence alumni over the past years since the program originated in Flora and all *their* parents. Then add all the instructors, the administrators, volunteers, and the music stores who make and provide the instruments and sell the sheet music and the recordings. It is impossible to know the exact number of people directly and indirectly connected to BSA, but by Ann Smith's rough calculations, all told it is at least a half million. That is her conservative estimate. If she were a dreamer, it would be two to three times that many.

"We will need to do something, Mr. Stolz," Sheely says. "You understand what this could mean for everything we've built if we permit this dilettante to go his own way. Every music teacher would come up with their own variations on our theme and start thinking they've found the holy grail. Before you know it, the Sequence will become watered down. Unrecognizable."

"Yes, that's what I am thinking. But he had been such a good boy. I don't really understand. But I suppose you're right."

"I'm sure of it, Mr. Stolz. Don't worry. I'll take care of this."

"That's what Ann Smith assured me."

"I'm not Ann Smith. I know how to get things done."

Two days later, Ballard Whitmore sits down to watch *Thursday Night Football* at his modest home in the quiet Sugar House neighborhood of Salt Lake City with his wife, Margie, and two children, the youngest only four months old. It has been a long day, and he just arrived home after stopping on the way from school for a takeout pepperoni pizza. Shortly after seven o'clock there is a knock on his door. In front of his wife and children, Salt Lake police officers pin Whitmore to the ground, handcuff him, and take him into custody, charging him with eighteen counts of sexual misconduct.

The next morning, *The Salt Lake Tribune* reported details of what led up to Whitmore's arrest, accusations of various forms of sexual abuse by four girls who played in the South High School orchestra. Being minors, the girls' names are withheld. Whitmore denied all the charges, calling them "absurd and untrue," and vowed to clear his name. He retained the services of a highly touted Salt Lake personal injury attorney, Richard Slyke, the father of a friend with whom he had gone to school, to represent him.

The school administration and parents expressed shock at the allegations, as Whitmore was one of South's most popular teachers and had been in the public spotlight for crafting the successful All Together music program. One parent, commenting what a personable gentleman Whitmore had always been, can't believe he is capable of committing such despicable crimes. Countering that, the *Tribune* quoted another parent as saying, "You can never tell who's going to be a wolf in sheep's clothing." The community is divided. The city quickly severs its connections with Whitmore. He is placed on administrative leave pending an investigation by the school district and the Salt Lake County district attorney's office. An individual count of sexual abuse of a minor, especially by an adult in a position of trust, is a third degree felony that could result in a multi-year prison term.

While the drama in Salt Lake City is playing out, Sandy Duckworthy is mixing business with pleasure in Fort Collins, Colorado, attending a BSA Intermountain Region conference. She steps out of her Coachman Hotel shower, which has much better pressure than hers at home in Flora, to get ready for her date with Darren Witten. Well, not really a date, but an interview, though you never know what it might turn into, right? She examines herself in the mirror. She is not displeased when men look at her. Though her figure is lithe and athletic, she isn't scrawny, like those emaciated marathon runners. She has breasts. When she skateboarded as a kid they'd called her a tomboy. But then, when she graduated to rock climbing and was the first woman to climb Artis Ledge unassisted, they started calling her "a physically gifted" athlete. That was when she was still a cub reporter at the *Daily Ledger*. Since then, she's filled out a little, but only in the places where it counts.

Duckworthy finishes dressing. Her outfit is tastefully revealing. She experiments with the number of buttons on her blouse to keep open. One more wouldn't hurt. Yes, that's better. Five minutes of makeup, which is five minutes more than usual. She heads down to the bar.

Duckworthy is at the conference to do a story on the BSA, already a burgeoning national phenomenon. She has a special affinity for this assignment. She likes to think that it was she—as a result of her glowing review of his first big concert—who initially had a hand in catapulting Layton Stolz to fame, without which boost he might have remained forever an unknown Flora curiosity. As one of his first big fans—she remembered the bouquet of daisies he sent her after her column—she would have attended the conference on her own time, since it was held nearby in Fort Collins and in a fancier hotel than she was used to. And, another plus, the beer is better in Fort Collins than in Flora. But there is also one other angle that has piqued her journalistic curiosity, for which she had to deftly manufacture an opportunity in order to address.

Darren Witten, a string bass player and an orchestra conductor in Evanston, Wyoming, is the recently-appointed director of the BSA Intermountain Region, which covers the vast geographical area but modest population of the Dakotas, Montana, Wyoming, Colorado, and Utah. Witten is one of the few African American administrators in the BSA, and a lot of publicity had been tossed in his direction as the organization touted its ongoing efforts to expand its demographic scope. Witten, personable, young, dynamic, and comfortable being around a lot of white folks, was Layton Stolz's handpicked choice for regional director. Entirely committed to the cause, he delivered a glowing keynote address at the conference, entitled *Noteworthy*, citing many of the accomplishments of state and local Sequence programs in the past year.

The workshop that intrigued Duckworthy the most on the conference's first day, called *Inspiring the Youth of Today*, was led by Layton Stolz himself. The BSA organizers, knowing it would be attended in huge numbers, held the event in the hotel's grand ballroom. Still, it was standing room only. Duckworthy, determined to make the most of the event, slipped into a front row seat next to Darren Witten before it was taken by—read the smiley face nametag—Wendy Simmons, Evanston, WY. "So sorry, Miss Simmons," Duckworthy said with a sympathetic smile. "Can I call you Wendy? Hope you don't mind, but I'm recovering from a knee injury. Skiing. Multiple fractures." An hour later, Duckworthy came out of the lecture mildly deflated, finding Stolz's talk understated and curiously uninspiring. She knows nothing about music, but it feels as if... As if? She searches for an analogy: If Leonardo da Vinci was Beethoven, Stolz's vaunted Sequence method is like learning to create the *Mona Lisa* with paint-by-numbers. But she kept that analogy to herself because everyone else gave him a standing ovation, so evidently she must have been wrong. The event did produce its intended reward, though. She had a date with Witten for an interview the next evening at eight-thirty after all the meetings were over, a time slot which on the conference schedule was designated as the Interactive Session.

"So let's get interactive," Duckworthy says, lifting her Belgian style ale that packs a 9.5% alcohol punch. Witten raises his Johnnie Walker Black.

"Here's to Layton Stolz," he says.

"And to Beethoven." Duckworthy winks.

"And to Beethoven, too."

Over the course of the next hour in the comfortably-appointed, dimly-lit Coachman Hotel lounge, Witten provides Duckworthy with a mound of information, much of it rehashed from the meetings she's attended and the pamphlets she has read: How efficiently the organization is structured, from the programs to the budget. How the BSA has the lowest percentage of administrative expenses of any nonprofit in the country. How it all goes to the kids. And look how we're thriving. He is giving her little that is new or, to coin his own phrase, noteworthy. But Witten does have nice eyes with long eyelashes, for a man, and a winning smile.

Witten is sipping his second scotch. She is on her third Belgian. She hopes he had loosened up as much as she has, enough so that she can ask about some past history, for which she has kept brief handwritten notes in her *Stolz, Layton* file.

"Do you recall Layton's"—my, how quickly she's gotten on a first-name basis with Stolz—"television interview with Diane Sawyer?"

"With the Long Island students? That was his first major break."

"Actually, that's not entirely accurate. *I* was his first big break." Leaning slightly forward, she points, not unintentionally, to her breast. "Not disputing it was thoroughly deserved. Yes, thoroughly deserved. What I want to know is, you know the Salt Lake guy Sawyer mentioned, this Ballard Whitmore, who wanted to do things his own way? Who started the music program called All Together? Arrested for sexually abusing four of his students? What do you know about that?"

"News to me. Haven't heard a word about that." Witten looks directly into her eyes. "You know you're a very attractive woman?"

She knows how she is going to answer that one. Because when Sandy Duckworthy was thirteen she got caught by Danny Amatucci in the act of stealing his state-of-the-art skateboard from his family's garage. Danny threatened to get her into trouble by telling on her to her parents, something she could hardly afford to allow to happen yet again. The previous time she had gotten into trouble had been a few months earlier when her older brother Andrew caught her sneaking away with a Hustler magazine he had stashed under his bed. Putting to good use the knowledge she had acquired from that experience, however, Sandy had said to Danny, a year her senior, "If you promise not to tell, I'll commit cunnilingus upon you." She wasn't totally clear about the terminology. Was it cunnilingus or fellatio? She couldn't remember, but the gist seemed to have gotten across.

"Well, okay," Danny said.

"And, you'll let me use your skateboard, too."

The deal was struck. Sandy pulled down Danny's pants and step by step carried out the procedure she had gleaned from the Hustler. The transaction was completed in less than a minute. Sandy, wiping her face with her sleeve, was delighted. Her freedom had been secured and she had gained unfettered use of the skateboard. Plus, she confessed to herself, the experience had not been totally unpleasant. But most of all, what she had learned from the Hustler instilled in her an abiding, lifelong respect for the value of accurate journalism.

A few years later she landed her first job at the *Flora Daily Ledger* as the local sports writer, which included everything from high school football to bowling tournaments at the Valley Mall Lanes. (She arrived too late on the scene to admire the exploits of Doug Stolz.) From there she moved up to arts and entertainment, covering school productions of *The Music Man* and a touring production of *Cats*. It was during that stint when she wrote her column about Layton Stolz and the *Egmont Overture*. After that story was picked up nationally, she received a promotion to fulltime staff as the features writer. From time to time, whenever she felt she merited a raise or a week's vacation, she was not averse to committing a kindness upon her editor.

So when Witten tells her how attractive she is, Duckworthy pretends to be the innocent, as if she doesn't get it he is deflecting the subject away from Whitmore. She pretends so well, short of batting her eyelashes, that she lets him pay for her beer.

"No, please. I couldn't—" she says.

"But I insist," he says. "Don't worry, it's on the conference account," he brags.

"I thought you said you've got a tight budget," she says. Maybe she is being too much of a tease. She can't really tell. The ale has definitely gone to her head.

"BSA Central cuts us regional directors a little slack. We do have some discretionary funds at our disposal."

"So you're being discreet?"

Duckworthy continues to feign innocence so well that she acts surprised when she ends up spending the rest of the night in the sack in Witten's hotel room. Why not? And she does learn some things, but not the things she could print in a local newspaper. Or anything about Ballard Whitmore, who remains strangely off limits. Every time Duckworthy even tiptoes toward Whitmore, Witten dances in another direction. She would have thought BSA would be crowing over the wayward son gone disastrously astray. Go figure. But the pleasantness of the evening compensates for her lack of headway into Whitmore. Witten does have those lovely eyes.

Duckworthy has filled her yellow legal pad with copious, mostly glowing notes of the two-day conference. Within the pages and interspersed with abstract, mindless doodles are occasional cautionary words like "brainwash," "mind control," and "1984 revisited," and the heavily-underlined name, Ballard Whitmore, followed by three question marks. But she keeps all of that out of her Sunday feature in the *Daily Ledger*, sticking to the overwhelming positives of the weekend. And, after all, wasn't it Layton Stolz who had put Flora on the map? So why not be charitable?

II

UTOPIA RAZED

Chapter Eleven

Ballard Whitmore doesn't mind living hard in grungy Room 201 at the Sunset View Motel, next to the boarded up Cash USA! pawn shop on South State Street. Rent by the week or the month. Since, with his minimum wage job, there is no way he can save enough to pay by the month, he rents by the week even though in the end it is much more expensive.

He blends right in with the shabby decor. Prison life—if you could call it life—has eroded his once athletic frame by almost twenty pounds. Much of the musculature that remains has lost its tone from long stretches of inactivity, resulting in a physique that is an incongruous combination of skinny with an emerging paunch. His face is pale and creased like his bed's poorly folded sheets, and his tawny brown hair is starting to ebb prematurely, both in color and quantity. His jeans, frayed at the cuffs and pockets, which he bought "pre-worn" at the Deseret Industries outlet for charity cases like him, is the snazziest item in his wardrobe. Secondhand clothes for a secondhand life.

Whitmore doesn't mind the racket the air conditioner makes when it randomly turns itself on and off, or the stained rust-colored shag carpet, pocked with the cigarette burns. He doesn't mind the room's mildewed dampness, or the dim ceiling light that flickers when trucks rumble by, which is often. He doesn't mind the toilet that runs constantly, with the indelible iron brown ring in the bowl, or the shower with its intermittent supply of spitting, scalding water. He doesn't mind the defective TV remote control that drains batteries faster than he can replace them. He doesn't mind the grind of the pickup trucks dragging down State Street through the night or the aimless meanderings of his motel's fellow residents, homeless folks placed there by various local agencies to help them "transition" back into the mainstream, or—more likely—back out of the mainstream. He doesn't mind the ranting drunks and drug addicts or the prostitutes' fake moans and beds banging against walls through the night. Nor does he mind his job washing dishes at El Chico's Mexican Grill eight hours a day, which at least gets him out of his room. His boss pays him under the table, which is fine with Whitmore, and will later be to his advantage, as it makes it possible for him to remain anonymous.

There is only one thing Ballard Whitmore does mind. The bedbugs, which makes sleep almost impossible. He wears a ski cap to bed and wraps a towel around the pillow, and showers every morning in an unending effort to drown any vermin that might have found sanctuary on or in his body over the course of the night, but even with those precautions he is only partially successful.

But after nine years of incarceration, even with the bedbugs, at least he is free from his cell and the other four-thousand inmates of the Utah State Prison at Point of the Mountain in Draper, Utah. And that's why he doesn't mind those other things.

He had been convicted of groping four underage girls. Of molesting them. Of unwanted touching of the breasts and genitals, both over and under clothing, and of nonconsensual kissing. His lawyer, Richard Slyke, noted to the court that there was simply no evidence he had done any of those things. None. There was no physical evidence of assault. No DNA evidence. No semen, no saliva, no hair. No bruising, no penetration. Whitmore's unblemished reputation had been stellar throughout his tenure at South High, and there never had been a single complaint against him. Except for the unaccountable words, only words, of four young ladies, there were no indications whatsoever that any of those alleged crimes had taken place. Slyke hoped that not only his arguments, but also his winning personality, would carry the day. He was one of those men whose faces would always be boyish even when their hair had turned white and their bellies overlapped their belts. One of those friendly faces that always seemed about to break out in a smile. Though he would never admit it to anyone other than himself, his personal charm had probably done more to win cases than his legal skills.

But words counted, the prosecution argued. The four girls' testimonies, taken independently, each corroborated the others' so consistently that it was almost inconceivable any one of them had fabricated the story. And why would they? By all accounts, these were four popular, honor roll students who had never been in trouble. What was there to be gained by false accusations? Nothing. To divulge such an experience was not only intensely painful in itself, the unfair social stigma of being a victim of sexual assault so often accompanied the unfortunate woman for the rest of her life. So why lie?

The prosecution had pointed to "the fact" that Whitmore went out of his way to "make himself attractive" to young girls. At times he was seen joking and laughing with them or working with them on their music after school. Slyke countered that this was Whitmore's behavior toward all his students, regardless of age or gender, not just the four girls. And that far from hiding that behavior, he espoused it. That's what All Together, the program so heartily endorsed by parents and school administrators alike, was all about. If the football coach behaved as Whitmore had, Slyke argued, he would be made coach of the year.

That's what makes Whitmore's behavior so insidious, the prosecution said. So easy to disguise. So easy to justify. But there was no hiding "the fact" that athletically-built, sandy-haired, blue-eyed Ballard Whitmore dressed more informally, "more youthfully" than many of the older faculty, in an effort, the prosecutors said, "to ingratiate himself with innocent, impressionable young girls," and lure them into his trust. To recruit them for his lascivious ends.

After two days of deliberation, the jury sided with the girls. At the sentencing, because Whitmore continued to maintain his innocence without expressing remorse for his actions, the judge handed down the maximum sentence permissible by law. The day after sentencing, Whitmore's wife, Margie, pregnant with their third child, filed for divorce and moved with their children to her parents' home in Boise, Idaho. Considering the circumstances, Whitmore couldn't really blame her. Shortly thereafter, the LDS Church, of which he and his family had been practicing members for generations, initiated excommunication proceedings. The church had long been under intense scrutiny for not being sufficiently proactive in its response to the sexual misconduct of a few of its male brethren. This was an open-and-shut case, and their unequivocal action would demonstrate their firm line for the world to see. They had little choice.

What bewildered Whitmore was: Why? What had he done to those girls that would make them turn on him? And with such a vindictive, coordinated attack? For the first four endless years of his incarceration, he had no idea. Then one day, a prison guard handed him a letter, postmarked four days earlier. He couldn't remember the last one he had received. Upon opening it, he saw it was from one of the girls who had accused him of abuse. She had been a flute player, the best in the orchestra, and one of his favorite students.

Dear Mr. Whitmore,
    I don't know how to say this other than I am so sorry. They made me do it. I know it has ruined your life, but it has also ruined mine.
    I am so sorry.
    Heather Hansen

The next day, Whitmore received permission to call his lawyer. He told Slyke he had something important to show him and arranged for a meeting at the penitentiary the following week. The two sat across from each other in a spare room, a bare table in between them. Whitmore slid the letter across the table to Slyke, who read it and slid it back.

"So?" Slyke said.

"What do you mean, 'so'?" Whitmore responded. "This letter exonerates me. 'They made me do it.' It proves that someone coerced those girls into perjuring themselves."

"And why would they do that?"

"I don't know, but is that really important? Isn't the important thing that she's recanting her accusations?"

Slyke pressed his eyes with his thumb and forefinger.

"What is it you want me to do, Ballard?"

"You have to go and interview Heather. After that letter, I'm sure she'll tell you the whole truth. She feels guilty. She wants to make amends. She'll come clean. I know it. She's a good girl."

"I'm afraid that won't be possible, Ballard," Slyke said.

"Why not? Is it the fee? I'll find the money."

"No. It's not the fee. It's not that at all." Slyke hesitated. "Clearly you have not heard the news."

"What news?"

"The day after she wrote this letter to you, Heather Hansen committed suicide. Ballard, this letter is a suicide note, and far from exonerating you, one might reasonably interpret it as you being responsible for her death, at least indirectly."

A black, spinning funnel encircled Whitmore, and he had to hold on to the edge of the table to maintain his balance. Heather, dead! He had convinced himself he was on the verge of vindication. Now he was shattered. Now he was truly grasping at straws.

"What about when she says, 'They made me do it'?" he asked. "What else can that mean other than someone was forcing her to lie?"

"It could mean many things, Ballard. You happen to believe 'it' means bear false testimony. Someone else could think 'it' refers to the abuse you were accused of committing. 'It' could also mean coming forward publicly, with 'they' being her parents, her friends, anybody, urging her to speak out. And you have to put yourself in her shoes. She was a confused, troubled young lady. Traumatized, stigmatized by the publicity alone, setting aside the abuse she suffered…allegedly. So troubled, in fact, that the day after writing this letter she took her own life. I'm sorry, Ballard, but my professional advice to you is to not show this letter to anyone. At best, it can do you no good. At worst, it has the potential of putting you into further legal jeopardy."

So far, this is Whitmore's lucky night. The remote control is working. He clicks on the television that's mounted high up, out of reach, in the corner of his motel room, chained to the wall to discourage the temptation to pawn it at Cash USA!

Whitmore is probably the only person within a radius of five miles who will be watching Rachel Maddow on MSNBC, but tonight's *Rapid Fire* segment is of particular interest to him. The show's skyrocketing ratings are at least partly attributable to the novel format. Guests have no prior knowledge of the questions, making prepared, practiced sound bites of little or no use. Maddow's questions come fast and furious. Viewers have witnessed the most hardboiled politicos crack under Maddow's withering interrogation. Tonight's guest is Layton Stolz, presidential candidate. Whitmore will watch the show attentively, and if he can summon up the courage, he will contact Stolz and ask—beg, if he has to—to return to the BSA fold. It is the only way Whitmore can think of to resurrect his career. His life. After what he had been accused of doing, and with his criminal record, who else would have the courage to hire him? Music was his life, and Layton Stolz had paved the way for him. Stolz had given him encouragement. Inspiration. He understood.

On one hand, Stolz's gradual rise to national prominence over the past nine years had been nothing short of miraculous. On the other hand, it had been entirely predictable. BSA had become so ubiquitous, it was vying with apple pie as *the* American icon. Then, the "Draft Layton Stolz" juggernaut had started with a seemingly innocent smattering of letters to the editor. The first one appeared in Wisconsin in the *Sheboygan Press*. Then the Selma, Alabama, *Times Journal*. Both letters had the same flavor. A cynic might have pointed out they were so similar they must have been planted by BSA's own people, but there was no way to prove that, and besides, how many people read both of those particular newspapers? "Layton Stolz should consider running for president," one the letters said. "Look what he's done for education." They cited new data indicating that U.S. public schools were now out-competing Finland and South Korea. "Look what he's done to reduce crime." More persuasive statistics.

When you throw a few kernels of Orville Redenbacher in the pan, as the oil heats up, the kernels pop. Then you add a third of a cup of the corn and in short order the popcorn starts bouncing off the inside of the pan like random machine gun fire. Those two letters were the first kernels. After a brief lull, the oil heated to the critical temperature, and the popping came hot and heavy. The BSA disavowed any concerted effort to put Stolz on the ballot. "These individuals wrote letters of their own volition, expressing their own personal views," their official statement said. "While Mr. Stolz appreciates the sentiment and warm thoughts of the American public, he has no intention of running for president of the United States."

But once started, there was no stopping the chain reaction. The message caught on like wildfire. Letters to newspapers and calls to radio talk shows flooded in by the thousands, along with rallies and marches with posters and banners and speeches, all begging Layton Stolz to run for president. What made Stolz's noncampaign so intriguingly effective was that he never declared what party he was a member of, because, in fact, he was a member of no party. The result was, none of his opponents knew what to attack or defend. What could they pin on Layton Stolz? All there was were the good deeds for which he had been universally credited. How could you attack that?

Still, Stolz shillyshallied. "Why on earth would I want to be president?" was his constant refrain when asked. What finally convinced him was Ann Smith laying out a vision, followed by a step-by-step strategic plan, of how he could use the presidency to further his goals of universal freedom through Beethoven. Like spreading the gospel. Stolz finally relented, submitting to overwhelming public sentiment, and announced his candidacy for president. He would not run as a Republican or Democrat. He would not run as a third party candidate. He would not even run as an independent. He would not run at all, per se, in the traditional sense. What he asked of America was simple: If you support what I stand for, vote for me as a write-in candidate.

Overnight, all the Sequence outposts, which had spread to hundreds of towns and cities in all fifty states, were converted seamlessly into campaign headquarters, staffed by devoted, ardent, steadfast, unwavering, resolute followers. Thousands of smiling, fresh-faced Sequence students, current and former, went door to door, spreading a quietly confident message of positivity and achievement. At Stolz's strict instructions, campaign literature (it was never referred to as campaign literature, but was always tied to BSA activities) was restricted to a few general subjects: the unquantifiable value of freedom and democracy, and of every citizen's individual responsibility to protect those precious gifts. And, of course, Beethoven. Stolz's simple message was trumpeted loud and clear; his opponents' were drowned out by Beethoven. Money and endorsements flowed in. The political machine ticked like a Swiss watch.

Meanwhile, Secretary of State Phillip Valentine's campaign for president had run aground like a glossy yacht with a defective compass. The lame duck administration with which he was associated had made promises intended to bolster the standard of living of the lower and middle class. Some of those promises had met with partial success, but what wins it had eked out weren't sufficient to trumpet with much fanfare because the losses balanced them out. Yes, the minimum wage had risen. That was good. But inflation had risen even faster, and that was bad, even though economists said administrations should neither be blamed nor given credit for macroeconomic swings, at least not entirely. During the campaign, Valentine had spoken eloquently and at length about improving race relations, but his track record was cast into doubt when he defended the actions of a policeman who had shot and killed an unarmed black youth. Responding to the public anger, which he underestimated for having taken that position, he then backtracked, saying he had been misunderstood, at which point he alienated the support of the so-called silent majority and the law enforcement community. As Secretary of State, Valentine had trumpeted his administration's Middle East peace plan, but in the end the trumpet went mute as that plan stalled out in the desert sand.

Valentine's main problem, though, was that he had no adversary to demonize. The grassroots movement to promote Layton Stolz's non-candidacy had already sucked the air out of Valentine's major party opponent, Vincent Lancaster, to the point that his party's leaders were rumored to be ready to pull the plug on Lancaster's campaign in order to then go ahead and endorse Stolz. But Stolz remained resolved neither to join a party, to campaign, nor to engage in debates or townhalls, regardless of who asked him.

"Why is my opponent afraid to debate?" came the desperate accusation from the Secretary of State. "What is he hiding from the American people?"

"People already know what I stand for," Stolz replied. "I don't need to repeat it every day. I'm too busy for that." The more stridently Valentine attacked Stolz, the more Stolz's poll numbers continued to climb.

For months, Valentine boxed with phantoms. It was like punching at feathers floating in the air. The hundreds of millions of dollars he had collected for his campaign war chest were doing him no good. In fact, all that cash contributed to his downward spiral, because in glaring comparison to Stolz's campaign budget, zero, it gave the impression—not without some validity—that Valentine was beholden to special interests while Stolz, clearly, was not.

The show begins, Rachel Maddow and Layton Stolz, both seated, facing each other in an otherwise empty studio. Nothing in between them. No table. No props.

"Welcome to *Rapid Fire*," Maddow says to the viewing audience. "Last week we heard from Secretary of State and presidential candidate Phillip Valentine. Now we welcome the most recent Time Magazine Person of the Year, Layton Stolz. Let's get right down to it. How much experience do you have in politics?"

"None."

"Don't you think that should disqualify you as a candidate for president of the United States?"

"Maybe. That's for the voters to decide."

"Looking at your background for a moment. You were a welder. You never went to college. Do you really believe you are qualified to be president?"

"No more than a news reporter."

"I'm not running for president."

"Maybe you should. You're probably more qualified than I am."

Layton Stolz makes a facial gesture that Whitmore believes is intended to be a smile, but looks rehearsed. Stolz must be uncomfortable, Whitmore thinks. And why not? He's such a private person, and all he cares about are Beethoven and teaching. Not histrionics.

"You're running as a write-in candidate. Some say that by doing that you're simply dodging the primaries."

"Yes, that's true."

"Wouldn't you say that can be construed as cowardice?"

"Yes, it can be construed that way. But that would be incorrect. I am apolitical, and frankly I have too much work to do."

"The FEC—Federal Elections Commission for the viewers out there—is investigating possible campaign law violations by your organization, the Beethoven Sequence Association. Spending millions of dollars of unacknowledged corporate donations to promote your campaign. What do you say to that?"

"There is nothing new here. Our philanthropists have been generous for many years. As a charitable organization our finances are subject to public scrutiny, which we welcome. All of our money goes to support our music programs. All of it. Look at the text of our donor requests. We have never asked for one dollar for a political campaign. If our various public communications make mention of the fact that I'm running for president…well, I see no problem with that. Besides, it's literally impossible we have broken any campaign finance laws."

"Why not?"

"Simply because I'm not campaigning."

"You're here tonight, though."

"Not my idea. You invited me."

Again, the twitch of a smile. It's almost like a mask.

"Let's move on to international relations for a moment. Do you feel qualified being the one with your finger on the nuclear button? Are you prepared for that?"

"I'll talk to our adversaries. I don't think it will come to that or anything close to it."

"Why not? What are you going to do? Play Beethoven for them?"

For a split second, Stolz's expression turns to, what? Rage? Yes, it's rage, Whitmore thinks. It's in his eyes. The rest of his face remains frozen in place. Whitmore stands up in front of the television set high so he can watch more closely. But as soon as he does so, Stolz's face returns to its standard, noncommittal passivity.

"It has often been said that music is the international language," Stolz replies. "On December 23, 1989, a month-and-a-half after the Berlin Wall fell, Leonard Bernstein conducted a concert of Beethoven's Ninth Symphony in West Berlin. Two days later, on Christmas Day, he led an identical concert across the border, in what was previously East Germany. The multinational orchestra included musicians from around the world, and both East and West Germany. Bernstein made one change to the symphony's text: instead of the word *Freude*, joy, the choir sang *Freiheit*, freedom. An *Ode to Freedom*. So yes, I would play Beethoven for them. And we would listen together. I believe that's why I'm getting as much support as I am. Sorry to be so longwinded."

"Why exactly are you running for the highest office in the land?"

"I believe in government's role to protect its citizens and to provide infrastructure."

"It is said you would eliminate welfare programs. Is that true?"

"Yes."

"Care to elaborate, candidate Stolz?"

"We wouldn't need them because everyone who wanted a job would get one that paid a living wage."

"And how would you accomplish that small feat?"

"Talk to employers and ask them to hire more workers at a living wage."

"Don't you think you're being a bit naïve?"

"Maybe. Though if certain businesses were not paying their employees adequately, I could perhaps persuade the public not to buy their products."

It might have sounded benign to most of the viewers, but to Whitmore the implicit threat is even more chilling, given its understatement.

"You would eliminate welfare, yet you seem to live quite comfortably. How much do you make per year as president of the BSA?"

"Last year, I made approximately $60,000, give or take."

"Are you prepared to provide your last five years of tax returns to back that up?"

"Yes. And because I've been asked that question many times, I've brought the past ten years. Here they are."

He hands them to Maddow.

"Well, thank you for that. We'll have our financial experts take a look."

"Please do."

"It's also been said you're anti-environmental protection."

"That's not true."

"But you say you'd cut out environmental programs. Is that true?"

"Yes."

"That sounds like a contradiction to me. Please elaborate if you don't mind."

"Everyone should take care of the environment. We should all be stewards of the land. Everyone should conserve. There is too much waste in America. Businesses should not pollute the air or water. They should not profit off of the things that make our world an unhealthy place. Again, they should realize that if they do pollute, I'll suggest the public not buy their products. It doesn't cost a cent to do this."

"Let's move on to immigration. You claim you would eliminate illegal immigration. How?"

"By making legal immigration easy and increasing the numbers exponentially."

"And I suppose you would require all new immigrants to learn to play Beethoven?"

"Not require. Invite. And we would provide free instruments to everyone, and they would play together with all other Americans, new or old."

Stolz sounds sincere. His sacred ground.

"Some of your orchestras have drowned out your opponents' voices when they've tried to speak. What do you say to that?"

"The Supreme Court has ruled that music is a form of speech and is protected under the First Amendment."

"That's what the Supreme Court says, but I asked you what *you* say to that?"

"I say that the voice of the common man has been drowned out by big government for far too long. What comes around, goes around."

This doesn't sound like Stolz. It's too rehearsed. Too political.

"I note that you said common *man.* Don't you include women in your philosophy?"

Stolz's face breaks into a smile, a rare and yet radiant occurrence, and so ingenuous that it's almost beatific.

"Ms. Maddow, how would you react if I referred to women as *common?*"

"Touché. Wrapping up here. You have not yet selected a running mate. Isn't it a little late in the game for that?"

"Yes."

"Have anyone in mind? Can we break the news to America on *Rapid Fire?*"

"Perhaps Phillip."

"As in Phillip Valentine? As vice president?"

"He'd make a good vice president, I think."

"That would certainly be a first. Which leads to my final question. What is your message to the American people why they should vote for you and not for Phillip Valentine?"

"If you think Phillip should be president, vote for him. If you think I should be president, vote for me."

The wooden smile, ephemeral, one last time.

"Fair enough, Mr. Stolz. Thank you for your candid, if unconventional responses. Certainly a different kind of candidate. And now a message from our sponsors."

Ballard Whitmore turns off the television and lies back in his insect-infested mattress, unmindful of the bedbugs. He is troubled. Deeply. There is something amiss. Stolz was the same. But different. His words echoed his past sentiments. Yes, that was the word. Echoed. A reflection of sound bounced off a surface. Hollow. Empty. His answers to Maddow's questions *sounded* like the real Layton Stolz. They reflected the kinds of things he would have said when Whitmore was a student. But now? Was it because

Whitmore was now older and world weary? Or was it because something had changed within Stolz. Something subtle, but at the same time insidious. His eyes betrayed an inner turmoil.

Whitmore gets no sleep. With new context, he relives his years in prison and what got him there, reassembling the pieces, the sequences. Reconsidering the events, the conversations. The motivations. The chronology. Especially the chronology. He loses count of the number of times he puts his head under the bathroom tap to stay awake. By dawn, haggard but no longer confused, Whitmore has reached an inevitable conclusion. He is not going to call Layton Stolz to ask for a job. No. Not Stolz. He is going to call Richard Slyke.

Chapter Twelve

The opulence of Richard Slyke's law office intimidates Whitmore, especially compared to the rathole he has been living in. The attractive, manicured receptionist who tries unsuccessfully to disguise her disdain for his appearance when he walks through the door. The dark wood paneling that has no semi-legible initials scratched into it. The framed degrees and family portrait on the walls instead of an ignored No Smoking sign. The long, polished mahogany conference table barren of empty Pop Tart boxes and pizza crusts. The works. And it is all a lot more expensive looking than the last time he was there, ten years ago. It is evident Slyke has hit the big time even though he lost Whitmore's case. Whitmore has brought the letter from Heather Hansen. The one that Slyke told him to hide five years ago. Before leaving the motel, he put the letter in a plastic sandwich bag, with only a few leftover crumbs in it, to keep it from getting wet. It was supposed to rain, but so far it was only cloudy. Slyke had been gracious enough to meet before Whitmore had to go to work at El Chico's.

"Now I understand what she meant, Richard. It was Layton Stolz. It has to be. It's the only thing that makes sense."

Layton Stolz is deranged, Whitmore has concluded. He will keep that to himself. For now. But is he the only one who can see it?

"Layton Stolz? How do you figure that, Ballard?" Slyke asks. Whitmore can already tell which side Slyke is on. Slyke is humoring him. Already planning on how to politely kick him out?

"The accusations the girls made came out two days after my KUER radio interview. Two days. And what was the essence of that interview? My

103

suggestion that the Beethoven Sequence was not the holy Bible. That going by the letter of the law—Stolz's law—was not as important as simply engaging students in something wholesome and creative. All Together. You get the same results. Better."

Slyke looks at him as if he's tempted to call security and have him escorted off the premises.

"Are you saying," Slyke replies, "that because you had a slightly different philosophy of music education from Layton Stolz, he bribed, or threatened, or extorted, four young ladies into bearing false testimony? To put their reputations on the line and claim publicly they were sexually abused? Don't you think you might be grasping at straws?"

"Not if Layton Stolz considers that anything that's not the word of Layton Stolz is blasphemy. Not when you look at the business model he set up. And now the political machine. Everyone has to be in lockstep with his program or you're out. Every gesture, every idea, almost every thought comes from on high. Richard, what would happen to BSA if someone like me were to have a different idea, and it worked just as well? Or better? The Beethoven Sequence is a house of cards, and if Layton Stolz lets one of those cards fall, the whole deck will collapse. Layton Stolz is scared to death of that. Layton Stolz is a fraud and his enterprise is a sham. He knows it and will prevent anyone from getting in his way."

"I hate to say this, but there are a few million very satisfied customers of this sham who would disagree with that statement. Layton Stolz is more popular than George Clooney and Tom Hanks combined. He may well be our next president. Ballard, I hate to tell you this, but Layton Stolz is virtually untouchable."

"But, Richard, look. You say my effect on his empire is small potatoes. But look what he did to me. To shut me up! Coerce those girls, then cover it up. If that ever gets out—"

"Ballard, there's nothing to 'get out.'"

"But—"

"And if you decide not to take my advice and go ahead and pursue this—and I say this as a friend as much as your attorney—you better make darn sure of" your facts, because otherwise the Stolz machine will chop you up into little pieces and flush them down the toilet."

Whitmore knows he should go to his dishwashing job—he's already late—but he's too shaken. He leaves Slyke's office—is the receptionist smirking when she wishes him a good day?—and walks around the block to take stock. Maybe Slyke was right, at least as far as cautioning him. After all, what he had been thinking was just so much speculation. He'll take his lawyer's advice and make darn sure of his facts, or at least come as close as he can.

He goes to the library. His plan? Call BSA, ask for a job, any job, and see where that leads. He knows there's no way they're going to let him talk to Layton Stolz directly, so, using the library's free computer, he Googles BSA and after a half hour finds Ann Smith's phone number. He calls on his old flip-top cellphone, which has no internet capability, hoping he'll be able to speak to one of her assistants.

A friendly young man answers. "Hi, I'm Randy." Whitmore identifies himself by name and in case that didn't set off alarms, reminds Randy he was one of Layton Stolz's first students at Flora High. He tells Randy his qualifications as a music educator, omitting mention of his nine years of incarceration. Randy thanks him and says he'll get back.

Whitmore leaves the library and is walking to work when his phone rings. He figures it's his boss, chewing him out for being late. Maybe he'll be fired. At this point he's not sure he cares. But it's not his boss. It's Layton Stolz. Whitmore is stunned.

"Hello, Ballard," Stolz says. "It has been a long time."

"Yes, it has, Mr. Stolz. Thank you for calling in person. I mean, I didn't expect you'd have the time."

"No problem, Ballard. Where are you living these days?"

Whitmore is about to say, in a dilapidated room at the Sunset View Motel in Salt Lake City, but then checks himself. An excess of caution, perhaps, after spending so much time in prison where trust was such a rare commodity and suspicion was the common currency. It just seems an odd question to Whitmore. Or at least out of place.

"Same old, in Utah."

There's a silence.

"Mr. Stolz? Are you there?"

"Of course. Of course. Utah. I have to say, I was very upset when you had to go through all that business."

"Business?"

"Well. You know. Anyway, I'm glad you're out. What has it been? Three months?"

"Yes. Three months."

"Good. Well, what can I do for you, Ballard?"

"I'm actually hoping to return to music, Mr. Stolz, and if there's a teaching job with BSA somewhere…"

"Oh, I know we could find something for you, Ballard. Yes, I'm sure of it. You'd have to pledge to do things the BSA way, of course. You do know that?"

"I understand."

"Good. I'm glad you understand. Well, let me see what I can find for you and we'll get back. Is that okay?"

"Yes. That would be fine."

"Good. And what did you say your address was?"

"Still in Utah."

Again the silence.

"Okay, Ballard. Well, it has been nice talking to you. And thank you for getting in touch."

Whitmore sleepwalks through the rest of the day. He does not remember arriving at work, whether his boss yelled at him for being late, or much of what he did until it was time for him to go home.

Returning to his motel room, Whitmore extracts a dog-eared Yellow Pages from the bottom drawer of the peeling, fake-wood desk. It is five years out of date, and its cover is scribbled with phone numbers. The name, *TANYA*, is scrawled in big capitals, accompanied by a crude graphic of a woman's genitals and a pair of breasts. Whitmore's thinking is that businesses still advertising in the Yellow Pages and not over the internet would be less expensive. And the smaller the ad, the cheaper yet. As he leafs through the alphabet, the pages between *Machine Tools* and *Mechanics* has been ripped out. Oh, well. No massage today. He does not have that kind of money to throw around, anyway. What money he does have is from the sale of his violin to a local instrument dealer, who paid him $12,000 even though it was worth twice as much. Sex offenders do not have much bargaining power. He put the money in the bank for his rainy day fund, and today it is pouring, both in his plans and outside.

P. Packing. Plants. Plumbers. Lots of plumber listings. His room could use a plumber. Ah! Here it is. *Private Investigators.*

Whitmore's phone call from Layton Stolz had sent a chill down his spine. He had hoped for a reaction from BSA, but that call had shocked him. First, that Stolz, in the midst of his presidential campaign, would call him personally about a simple job application; second, that he would ask, not once but twice, where he lived; and third, that Stolz knew that he had been out of prison for three months. Whitmore hadn't told anyone—in fact, he kept it as much a secret as he could—and he knew with fair certainty that, if his release had been noted at all in the media, it would have been no more than a paragraph on page eight of the local section.

There are not many listings for private investigators. Here's one. Stavros Santos. No big ad, no come-on. Only a phone number. Whitmore calls it. Santos answers it. Himself. No receptionist. A good sign. Low budget. They set up an appointment. Whitmore hangs up.

He goes into the bathroom and looks into the cracked mirror. His face is dull, worn beyond its years. Am I the insane one? he asks the face in the mirror. Am I paranoid? Layton Stolz has just personally offered me a job, and I'm afraid to even tell him where I live? Did nine years in prison make me like this? Was I like this even before that? Is it possible I really did molest those girls? No, that can't be.

As has become his habit, he washes his face in cold water and dries it with a ragged towel. He'll wait to see what kind of offer he gets from BSA and take things one day at a time from there.

Santos has his office on 500 South, across from the old city library, on the second floor above Ace Bail Bonds. Whitmore feels right at home. The office is almost as seedy as his motel room. Sitting at his desk, Santos is a big man in a small suit. Maybe at one time it fit him, but the Arby's next door is no doubt grateful for Santos's close proximity. With beady eyes like black marbles, continuously scanning, thinning hair close-cropped, and an old-fashioned walrus mustache, he could be a gendarme in an Inspector Clouseau comedy. Whitmore hopes Santos will be more competent than that.

"What may I do for you?" Santos asks, hands folded. His name, appearance, and accent suggest Greek or Balkan ancestry. Santos's grandfather, after whom he had been named, was, in fact, among the early non-Mormon settlers who made Utah home, emigrating from the Greek island of Corfu to work in the coal mines in the Book Cliffs area around Price. The tales of justice denied to immigrants that he related to his grandson spurred young Stavros on to visions of a career in law. But, without the necessary funds for his education, he became a private eye, his alternate route to seeking justice. Not as grandiose, perhaps, nor as lucrative for sure, but it did have its occasional rewards. And it paid the rent.

Whitmore provides Santos a concise, rehearsed summary of his situation. It is all truthful, painfully truthful at times, and when it diverges from fact to his personal opinion, he says so. If he is going to scale the mountaintop and take down Layton Stolz, his base camp will have to be on firm ground.

"Thank you for the background," Santos says when Whitmore finishes the backstory. "Coffee?"

"No, thanks."

"I see. Mormon?"

"Used to be."

"I understand. So what do you want me to do for you?"

"I want you to find proof why Heather Hansen lied about me."

"And how do you want me to do that?"

"I don't know! I'm not the detective. You are."

"Mr. Whitmore, maybe you've been watching too many movies on Netflix. So let me educate you a bit about what private investigators do in real life, if you don't mind. I'd say a good seventy-five percent of our time is spent sitting in a car opposite someone's house, with a camera, waiting for a door to open. When the door does open—*if* it does—we take pictures and provide them to the client, aka the spouse. Our job is done. What they do with those pictures—whether they take them to their lawyer, or show them to their spouse, or God forbid do something violent—is none of our business. The other cases, the other twenty percent of the time, we do internet searches, doing background checks for arrest records, back payments, debts, contact information. Most of this kind of stuff any private citizen is capable of doing on his own with a little effort and for about five dollars, but we don't tell them that. So when you ask me to delve into a closed case that's ten years old to search for something that may or may not be there in an effort to bring down a highly popular presidential candidate, you're asking for something somewhat above my pay grade."

"What about the other five percent?" Whitmore asks. "Seventy-five plus twenty equal ninety-five."

"The remaining five percent would be lunches, Mr. Whitmore."

"Could you just see what you can do?" Whitmore asks.

Santos must have heard something in Whitmore's voice. Hopelessness, maybe. Despair. Desperation. Something. Honesty?

"Okay, Mr. Whitmore. Okay. I'll nose around. But don't call me. I'll call you. And if I don't find anything, it's on the house. But don't get your hopes up."

The next day, Whitmore receives a phone call. It's from the Intermountain Region BSA office.

"Mr. Whitmore?" Another friendly voice. Female this time.

"Speaking."

"I'm happy to inform you that we'd like to offer you a job!"

Whitmore is elated. For a moment. Then he's suspicious. Is my paranoia kicking in again? He kicks himself, but remains cautious.

"What sort of job?"

"Well, at first it's an office job, because, well, you know…"

Whitmore understands.

"I understand."

"But then, you know, if everything works out..."

"Where's the job and when do I start?"

"Well, before we go there, we need to send you some forms to fill out. What's your current address, please?"

Whitmore hangs up.

A week passes. He hasn't heard from Santos. Or BSA. Certainly, with their tentacles they would be able to find out his whereabouts. All they'd have to do is call his parole office. Maybe when he hung up on them, they said good riddance to bad rubbish. Forget him.

Two weeks pass. Three. A lot of dirty dishes at El Chico's. A lot of looking over his shoulder.

"I've got something," Santos says over the phone. "Maybe. Come down to the office when you have a chance."

Once again seated across from Santos, Whitmore is on edge. He senses a breakthrough is imminent. Santos places a photo, copied from *The Salt Lake Tribune*, facing him. He recognizes it immediately.

"Can you identify the persons in this photo?" Santos asks.

"Of course! Those are the four girls that accused me. This photo must be over ten years old."

"Can you tell me their names?"

"You know their names!" Whitmore cries. "Is this all you've found in three weeks? A ten-year-old newspaper photo?"

"Please be patient, Mr. Whitmore. I just need to do this step by step."

"Okay. There's Heather Hansen in the middle," he says, pointing to the teenage girl holding her flute because the photo has been taken after one of their spring festival concerts, a year before the horror. Heather Hansen. Deceased. It gives Whitmore pause. "On the left is Kimberlea Heath. She played flute, too, but not as well. Next to her is Lexi Briscoe, who played harp, and the one on the right is Joy Sparks, who played clarinet. Do I pass the test?"

"No need to be sarcastic, Mr. Whitmore. Believe me, I do appreciate your desire to move forward. Now, Mr. Whitmore, can you tell me why these

110

four girls were photographed together?"

"What do you mean? They were in my orchestra."

"But why just the four of them and not any others?"

"Well, I guess it's because they were best friends. That's probably why."

"Aha. Good observation. That's what I gathered from this photo as well."

"Why is that important? They chose to reveal their names at the trial. Everyone knows who they were."

"Yes, and I did trace their current addresses and thought about calling each one of them, the three surviving ones, Mr. Whitmore, to ask them to delve back into the past and maybe reconsider their testimony."

"Yes, I would hope so. That could be the key."

Santos narrows his eyes and looks directly at Whitmore.

"But are you saying you didn't?" Whitmore asks.

"In the end, I decided not to. The reason is that the young teenagers in this photo—except for Miss Hansen—are now all married with children. Mothers with families. And as far as I could ascertain, leading normal, happy lives. I concluded that the chance of them changing their story at this point in time was negligible given their current circumstances, and if one of them did, it could ruin their lives."

"So we're at a dead end?"

"Not necessarily. I want to show you a couple more photos."

Santos pulls open the center drawer of his desk with some difficulty, because it is stuck, and manages to extract four more photos. He places them side by side, facing Whitmore. The one on the left is of a girls' soccer team. Next to that is a photo of Whitmore with a group of orchestra students, including the four girls, all holding their instruments. The third photo is a group picture from the South High yearbook in which those four girls looked a little older. The photo on the right seems to be a party of some sort, maybe a Sweet Sixteen or a prom, with boys and girls—they're all dressed up with corsages and holding hands—which must have been taken shortly before the horror began. All four girls are present in that photo, too. Unfortunately, none of the photos have captions with names of the individuals.

"So?" Whitmore asks.

"Look carefully, Mr. Whitmore. Sometimes the most obvious thing gets overlooked because one's mind is patterned to think along narrow, predetermined lines. What do you see? Look at each one, from the earliest to the latest."

Whitmore sits there, befuddled, for what seems an interminable amount of time, trying to analyze every detail of each photo for the clue that seemed so obvious to Santos. Finally, when he sees it, he sits up with a start.

"Aha! Mr. Whitmore. Tell me what you see."

"Each photo has a group of kids. They're a different group in each, except for..."

"Yes, except for how many girls?"

"The four girls who accused me. And one other."

"Exactly, Mr. Whitmore. And now we must find the fifth girl, for she may hold the key."

Much to Santos's disappointment, Whitmore only vaguely recognizes the fifth girl and can't remember her name. It had been too long ago, and with so many students it was impossible to get to know them all. She was probably one of the quiet ones. The next day, Santos drives to the Granite School District administration office, where they have archived school yearbooks dating back to the 1920s. On the South High School shelf, he starts with the yearbook from when Whitmore was accused of misconduct and proceeds from there. He finds the girl's graduation photo two yearbooks later. Her name is Samantha Summerhays. Returning to his office, he does an internet search, discovering there are five Summerhays residences in the neighborhoods that could have sent children to South High. Santos calls each one. None of them turn out to be Samantha's address, which does not surprise him, as it had been so many years. One of the Summerhayses who answered Santos's query, however, is a second cousin of Samantha's father and had heard that Randall Summerhays and Mrs. Summerhays, Norma Lee, had moved from their Salt Lake City neighborhood some years ago. Being distant relations, they weren't all that close, so he couldn't remember precisely how many years ago they had moved or where Randall and Norma

Lee had moved to.

Santos perseveres, making the fairly safe assumption Samantha's family were members of the LDS Church. They had lived in a predominantly LDS neighborhood and Summerhays was a fairly common LDS name, so he contacts the bishop of the LDS ward whose constituency includes that neighborhood. Santos grudgingly admires the church official's effectiveness at stonewalling his efforts to find information about members of his flock. Santos, not being a member of the church, asks Whitmore for some advice. At his suggestion, Santos finds out all he can about the parents on the internet and stands outside the Summerhayses' former local ward on the next Sunday, as services let out. Claiming to be an old friend from Idaho who had been out of touch for many years, he talks to one member of the congregation after another about what wonderful people Samantha's parents were, asking if anyone knew where they had moved to.

His questioning is met with responses ranging from suspicion to polite smiles, but with no actionable intelligence. About to give up, he finally receives a positive response from a middle-aged woman named Brecklyn Roberts who manages to maintain a brilliant smile even as two blond toddlers tug at her skirt.

"Oh yes, I remember the Summerhayses. They lived next door," she says. "I used to babysit for their daughter, Samantha. She was so easy to tend. Quiet girl. Gosh, they were super nice!"

"Do you know where I can find Samantha? Or her family?"

"I don't know what happened to Samantha after high school. I think she went on a mission. Her family, I think moved to Washington Heights."

"New York City?"

Brecklyn laughed.

"No, Washington Heights near Saint George, Utah! It's a mobile home community."

"Thank you very much," Santos says. He is beginning to be encouraged. "I'll just give them a call, then."

"That might not be so easy," Brecklyn said.

"No? Why not?"

"I heard they mightn't have a phone. As if they wanted to live off the grid. I think that's the reason they moved."

Santos calls the manager of Washington Heights Mobile Home Park and asks whether Randall and Norma Lee Summerhays still live there. Yes, they do. And could the manager please give them a message from an old friend?

"Sorry, bud, I'm not an answering service. They got rid of their phone for a reason. If you want to talk to them, you'll have to do it in person."

"It's a four-and-a-half hour drive, Ballard." Santos, the pragmatic realist. "Three-hundred-one-point-nine miles. One way. If you want me to go, it will have to be on your dime, not mine. For my time, for gas, for mileage. Or you could go yourself. Up to you."

Whitmore does not own a car. He could rent one, of course. But once he introduces himself as Ballard Whitmore, the infamous Ballard Whitmore, the Summerhayses will undoubtedly slam the door in his face. And the money! He is running out of it and Santos's meter is ticking.

Santos is not unsympathetic to Whitmore's struggle. He thinks of his grandfather, Stavros, whose dedication to justice he has always tried to emulate. Justice comes at a cost. He just wishes it wasn't always his.

"I tell you what," he says. "If it's a bust, you don't pay. But if we get somewhere, the trip goes on the tab. Discount. But I will need you to come along with me. Something might come up where I'll need a quick answer. Who knows? Deal?"

The next morning they are southbound on I-15 early, before rush hour will slow them down to a crawl and make a long day even longer. And, as most of the traffic is coming northbound into the city, it's not too bad at all.

They drive for two hours, passing Provo and then Nephi. Cruising past fields in the foreground and mountain ranges in the distance, traffic has thinned to a trickle. There will be no more significant traffic or population until their destination.

Santos says, "Don't turn around, but there's a silver Acura about a half mile behind us."

"So what?"

"I think it's the same one that was behind us back in Salt Lake."

"That's not such a surprise. I-15's the main route north to south."

"Except I've been driving under the speed limit, and everyone else is doing the limit or above. Everyone except him."

"Why would anyone be following us?"

Santos shrugs and switches on his turn signal.

"What are you doing?" Whitmore asks. "This isn't our exit."

"Watch and learn."

Santos pulls off the freeway at the Santaquin exit and stops at the top of the off ramp. There he waits for a good five minutes. If the Acura had been following them, it would definitely have gotten off the exit by now. He puts the car back into drive and returns to the freeway.

"You may think I'm a little paranoid. But one can't be too cautious."

An hour later they see the car again, this time ahead of them, as they approach Cedar City.

"Either I'm coocoo for cocoa puffs, or this guy is a real pro," Santos says.

"How are you going to find out?"

"Stay behind him the rest of the way. If he keeps going after we get off at Washington Heights, I'd say we're in the clear."

They keep an eye on the Acura for another hour, until they get off the freeway at Exit 13 for Washington Heights. The Acura in front of them continues south toward Saint George without slowing down.

"So much for being followed," Whitmore says.

"You hope."

They wend their way through the mobile home community along Buena Vista Boulevard, through North Main Street to Huntington Hill Road.

"Pretty nice," Santos says. The surroundings are a lot more pleasant than the image of a rundown RV cluster off in some backwoods, inhabited by survivalists and surrounded with rusted-out cars and snarling dogs, which is the image Santos had conjured when he learned the Summerhayses were off grid. The houses here, though uniformly modest, are for the most part tidy and in good condition. The Summerhays home is no exception. A double-wide with a peaked roof and lime green vinyl siding, the house looks comfortable, even inviting. Santos reminds himself that one of these days he should wash the dishes wallowing in his apartment sink. The Summerhays front yard is all gravel with a collection of a dozen or more lawn gnomes scattered about, and, with the local climate more an extension of southern California than of Utah, the palm tree in front of their home is not out of place.

Santos parks a block away and walks to the house. Whitmore elects to remain inside the car. If the Summerhayses recognize him from his photos in the newspaper, their whole effort will be wasted. Santos, standing on a mat that says WELCOME in big letters, knocks on the front door.

"Who's there?" comes the guarded voice of an elderly man. False advertising?

"Mr. Summerhays? My name's Santos. Stavros Santos. I'm a friend of Brecklyn Roberts."

There is no answer.

"She used to babysit for Samantha."

The door opens. An elderly couple, not dissimilar in appearance to the couple in American Gothic, but without a visible pitchfork, stands before Santos.

"How did you say you know Brecklyn?" Summerhays asks.

Santos uses their off-grid existence to his advantage. Chances are they have no idea whether or not he is telling the truth.

"I've done some remodeling on Brecklyn's house. Their kids are getting so big. And now with the two little darlins! Ah! Those blue eyes! They needed more room."

"And so what do you want with us?"

"Shouldn't we ask Mr. Santos in, Randall?" Mrs. Summerhays says.

"First I want to know what he came all the way from Salt Lake for. Then I'll invite him in. Maybe."

"Oh!" Santos improvises smoothly. Suspicion goes with the territory. "I was just passing through, really. I'm on my way to Mesquite for a home remodeling convention, and thought, well, I would just stop by and say hello for Brecklyn."

"Consider it done, then," Summerhays says, and begins to close the door.

"Randall, please!" Mrs. Summerhays says. "Do come in, Mr. Santos. We don't get visitors very often, so we're a little out of practice. Aren't we, Randall?"

Santos sits in an overstuffed, frilly easy chair and sips orange drink to wash down an overly-sweet chocolate chip cookie. Mortimer, a yellow tabby cat as filled out as the easy chair, rubs against his ankles. Santos goes on at length about Brecklyn and her family. Norma Lee Summerhays is pleased to hear that the house renovation should be finished under budget and ahead of schedule. He finally gets around to mentioning that Brecklyn was interested in reconnecting with Samantha, wanting to find out how she was doing after all these years. That subject elicits a much different response. Mrs. Summerhays begins to cry.

"I think it's time you left, Mr. Stavros," Randall Summerhays says. "You've upset my wife."

Santos apologizes profusely and asks, "Is Samantha not well? What would you like me to tell Brecklyn?"

"We have no contact with our daughter, Mr. Santos. For years. She went on a mission and never returned. And we're glad she stayed away."

"Please, Randall," Norma Lee pleads. But Randall is piqued and will not be stopped.

"She changed her religion while she was at it, and embarrassed and shamed my wife and me in the process. We became victims of a whispering campaign among people we thought were our friends, who decided we had failed as parents. We were ostracized by our neighbors, but even then, the anonymous, hateful calls never stopped. That is why we left Salt Lake City and why we don't particularly appreciate strangers showing up unannounced at our doorstep."

Mrs. Summerhays says, "I'm very sorry, Mr. Santos," and leaves the room.

"I'm sorry to have caused all of this upset, Mr. Summerhays," Santos says. "I truly am."

On his way out the door, Santos says, "And you said Samantha's mission was to Argentina?"

"No, I didn't. It was to Ireland. And a good day to you, sir."

The door slams behind him.

Back in the car, Santos tells Whitmore about the conversation. Next stop, Ireland. No, not really. But at least some research. And it is progress, and possibly significant.

"And I have something that might be of interest to you," Whitmore said in response.

"Really? Like what?"

"Like while you were inside, a silver Acura drove past."

Chapter Thirteen

"When you elect me president of these United States," Phillip Valentine proclaims, "I will finish the job we've started. The job of making the American dream a reality for all, not just the rich and powerful!"

Valentine's rambling press conference at an urban development center in Flint, Michigan, has been dragging on much longer than would have been advisable for a confident candidate. As his poll numbers decline, the decreasing number of straws at which he grasps are becoming increasingly, desperately brittle. Yet, grasp he does, employing a throw-it-against-the-wall-and-see-what-sticks strategy to woo voters. He lays out his new plan, Renew America, promising to purify the tainted local water supply, promising to provide jobs—high-paying manufacturing jobs, no less—promising interest-free home mortgages, promising college scholarships for all people of all races, and promising to increase Social Security benefits. He promises to clean up the corrupt and inefficient bureaucracy at our veterans hospitals so all of America's heroes who have placed their lives in harm's way on the battlefield to keep our country free will receive the same quality of care as the members of Congress. He promises to provide lifetime free healthcare for first responders, and promises to heal the growing rift between the public and the police, or as he calls them, officers of the peace. He promises equal pay for women and six months of paid maternity leave. That covers just about everyone and everything, or so he hopes.

With the promises out of the way, Valentine sharpens his attack on Layton Stolz. "And what will my opponent do for America? No one knows, because he continues to refuse to debate. Why won't he debate? Because he makes promises he can't keep. Because he's scared. That's why. Americans don't run scared or run from adversity. Americans stand and fight."

Valentine saves the bombshell for last. Stewart Wolfe, his top aide and fixer, has cautioned him against mentioning it: the contents of the letter that arrived on Wolfe's desk only two days before. It is more than a risk. It could sink his candidacy. But at this point, he desperately needs to poke his stick deep into the hornet's nest, even if it means he might be stung.

"Mr. Secretary," Wolfe said.

"What is it?" Valentine asked.

"We got a letter from some guy out in Salt Lake City."

"Who gives a shit? Utah is not going to win an election for me."

"It's just that he says he has some information about Layton Stolz that you might be interested in."

"What information?"

"He says he was framed by Stolz."

"What?"

"It got him sent to prison."

"When?"

"Nine years ago."

"Nine years? Shit. Nine days would be better. What's his name?"

"Whitmore. Ballard Whitmore."

"Okay. Do a background check."

"We did. The guy's a registered sex offender. He molested little girls."

"Fuck."

"Should we forget about it?"

"Yes." Then Valentine considered the poll numbers. "Maybe. For now. Keep his name on file. But don't respond to him. Can you imagine what the press'll say if they find out we're working with a perv?"

"All right."

"Wait a second. Does he have any proof Stolz framed him?"

"Not yet, but he said he's working on it."

"Shit."

"I'll tell you why Layton Stolz is scared," Valentine says. He takes a deep breath and makes an attempt to look sincere and deadly serious. "We have reason to believe that my opponent, Layton Stolz, was involved in a lurid sex scandal that sent an innocent man to prison."

The reporters, who had been trying, mostly unsuccessfully, to think of something new to write, now have fresh meat. Hands shoot up. A roar of questions.

"We're gathering the facts and will have more soon," Valentine says. "Thank you. That's all for now."

He does not take any questions.

You nailed it, Mr. Secretary," Wolfe says after he leaves the podium. "Your timing was impeccable."

"Any word from this Whitmore sicko?" Valentine asks. "The clock's ticking. If we don't get something from that asshole soon, I'll throw him under the bus."

"They're still looking for the fifth girl, sir. But they've at least got a name now and know where she is. It shouldn't take much longer."

"It better not. And you make damned sure it isn't. And it better not be known we're communicating with a sex offender, or you'll be next to Whitmore under the bus."

Chapter Fourteen

"Paddy and Johnny Boy, you run off to school now or you'll be late, and you know how your bum will feel about that!"

As her two children bob down the narrow, hawthorn-lined lane, she spies two men approaching them from the opposite direction. A rare occurrence in her out-of-the-way corner of the world. She keeps a maternal eye on them. Laurel and Hardy, those two men, she thinks with a wary smile. She can tell immediately both of them are Americans. They have that look. Indefinable, but definite. The tall, thin one, the shabbily dressed one; he seems nervous, looking over his shoulder, trying to find something? The shorter, dumpier one, the one with the big mustache; he's calmer. Wearing a suit that's too tight. She can't remember the last time she had seen a man wearing a suit and tie. Easy enough to tell they aren't Irish. They're walking too fast on such a pleasant day and show no appreciation for the fine autumn colors or the fresh breeze coming off the sea. Yes, they're American. She knows that because…well, just because. Her two children stop as they're about to cross paths with the men, who begin to talk to them. The fat one, Hardy, kneels down to the kids' level. Too far away for her to hear anything that's said, but little Johnny Boy turns and points up at her, at their house on the hill. Hardy pats Johnny Boy on the head, after which her two children hightail it down the lane at double speed, her admonition about being late no doubt still ringing in their ears.

Bucolic Sheep's Head Peninsula on the southwest tip of Ireland might be one of the world's most tranquil places. Beyond the hamlets of Durrus and Ahakista, the last coastal village before you wade into the Atlantic

Ocean, is Kilcrohane. Yes, tourists come and go—her hilltop B&B depended on them—but that's the world today, isn't it? During the period, the media dubbed the Celtic Tiger—Ireland's economic "miracle" of the '80s and '90s—ill-advised apartment blocks on the outskirts of town sprouted like dandelions and were equally unsightly. When the bubble burst, they remained unfinished and unoccupied, like abandoned doll houses. Other than that, though, Kilcrohane hadn't changed much over the last three- or four-hundred years.

Laurel and Hardy don't have the look of a honeymoon couple in search of the secluded charm of a quaint Irish B&B. Approaching her home, they look more like determined men on a mission, and she has a premonition of what the mission is. There is nothing she can do about it. Yes, there is one thing she can do. She fills the black iron kettle with water. An ancient relic from leprechaun times bequeathed to her by her house's previous owners, she lugs the two-stone kettle to the stove to make tea.

A knock on the front door, which is wide open, as always.

"Samantha McCollum?" Hardy asks, with an accent not quite American. But American enough.

"That will be me. And you are?"

"Santos. Stavros Santos. And this is my friend, Ballard Whitmore. We're Americans."

They are no longer Laurel and Hardy. She looks at Whitmore. She would not have recognized him, he has changed so. Yes, it has been more than a decade, but he has aged faster than that. Like a withering apple that hangs unpicked on the tree after a hard frost. When she saw them coming up the lane, she had not anticipated it would actually be him, in person. She doesn't know how she should respond.

"Well, come on in. Tea is almost ready."

They sit at the heavy, hand-hewn wooden table into which some clever medieval craftsman had hammered wrought iron corners to prevent wear and tear. They chat about the quaint Irish countryside and the magical charm of the villages. The potato famine. The pubs.

"More tea?"

The folk music. The mackerel fishing. The story-telling. The ancient stones whose mysterious origins or meaning no one understands for sure. That's why they're mysterious, right? They drink more tea and eat Irish currant scones with clotted cream. She pretends she doesn't know Whitmore. It is a subterfuge she is reasonably sure will not last, but why take chances? Maybe the storm cloud will go away, as they all do sooner or later.

It doesn't.

After the two men thank her for her hospitality and she has cleared the dishes, the cloud only darkens.

"Mrs. McCollum," Santos says, "can you please verify that your family name is Summerhays and that you were born and raised in South Salt Lake, Utah? In the United States?"

In her heart, Samantha McCollum knew this day was going to come. As a teenager, she had left Utah to go on a mission, as many Mormon girls do. Eighteen months away from home, isolated from family and friends, knocking on strangers' doors in a foreign land. The difference between Samantha and most other youths who went on a mission was that she had not been religious at all, and from the time she was a toddler, her parents had to coax and bribe her to go to Sunday services. So they were pleased, if puzzled, when she had asked to go on a mission, as unlike the situation for boys, it is not nearly as compulsory for a girl. If a boy doesn't go on a mission, eyebrows are raised. Questions are discreetly asked. Parents are viewed harshly. If a girl doesn't go on a mission, it just means she'll continue her education while keeping an eye out for a husband. An equally noble endeavor.

As a youngster, Samantha rarely prayed. But when she applied for her mission, she prayed in earnest. She prayed that the church elders, in their wisdom, would send her somewhere remote. Somewhere distant. Her prayers were answered. Samantha Summerhays was sent to County Cork in Ireland. When her eighteen months were up, her mission partner—for they always proselytize in pairs—returned to Utah and enrolled in Brigham Young University, more or less predetermining her future domesticity. But Samantha stayed. It was the right place for her to be, far from what had happened, in a corner of the world where the people she left behind would have a hard time finding her. That was the reason, the sole reason—which she had never told another soul—why she had gone on the mission. Then, to put the past even farther behind, she married, changing her last name, becoming an Irish citizen. She even changed her religion. Why not? It was all the same hocus-pocus, anyway.

Her husband, Malcolm, was at his office job in Skibbereen. He wouldn't be home until dinner. He didn't know anything. But now he'll have to find out. She'll have to tell him. It will be all right. She'll cook him a roast with three veg. It will be all right.

She nods in response to Santos's question.

"Well, you've found me," Samantha says. "It's not been any secret, my whereabouts. You make it sound like I've been in hiding." She's lying, and knows it.

"I'd suggest otherwise," Santos says, and summarizes their efforts to find her.

She looks into Ballard Whitmore's haggard eyes. He returns her gaze, without blinking. They are not happy eyes. That much she can easily tell. But are they angry? Puzzled? Vengeful? What can he be thinking? We'll find out soon enough, though. Of that she is all but certain. Secrets don't last forever, do they? She had played cello in his school orchestra a lifetime ago. The cello went into the closet the day after it all happened and never came out again. They were both different people now. As far as she was concerned, their former lives had never existed.

"Now that you've explained how you found me," she says, "you might want to explain the reason for making such an expensive trip. Surely it wasn't for tea and scones."

"Eleven years ago," Whitmore says. Then he stops. He stops and chokes, the words lodged in his throat like a chicken bone. He tries to clear it, but he can't get a sound out. Is there a Heimlich maneuver for words?

"Water?" she asks.

He nods, and points to Santos.

"You talk," he manages to say. "You talk and I'll listen."

"Eleven years ago," Santos says, taking over, "four teenage girls, Heather Hansen, Kimberlea Heath, Lexi Briscoe, and Joy Sparks, accused my client, Mr. Whitmore, of sexual misconduct."

Whitmore shakes his head forcefully. "Not accurate," he says, barely above a whisper. But the anger is there.

"Pardon me," Santos says, "*falsely* accused my client of sexual misconduct. We believe you might be able to help us understand why."

"Might I ask why you think that?"

"You were in the orchestra with the other girls. Circumstantial evidence suggests you were close friends with them."

"They had lots of friends."

"I'm sure they did. But still. Here we are. We think you can shed some light. In fact, from the great lengths we've come to find you, you can infer we believe you and only you can shed some light."

He lets that statement linger in the air, like a string of yarn in front of his cat, Archie. The cat might sit there one minute, two, more, but eventually it wouldn't be able to resist temptation and would leap at it.

Samantha keeps her eyes riveted on Whitmore.

"And if I told you I know nothing that can help you?"

"Then we could only conclude one thing," Santos says. "That it was you who, for some reason we don't know yet, coaxed your friends into falsely accusing Mr. Whitmore of sexual misconduct."

"I did no such thing."

"Then who did?"

"I don't know. I have nothing to say."

Santos keeps his voice low, but leans forward just enough to communicate a new level of seriousness, if not intimidation.

"Are you aware that out of remorse for what she had done to Mr. Whitmore, Heather Hansen killed herself? Did you know that?"

Santos has shocked her. Samantha McCollum puts her mug of tea on the table so she won't spill it. But she is not in full control of her muscles, and the mug lands with a bang.

"I don't believe it."

126

From his pocket, Santos pulls the suicide note Heather Hansen wrote to Whitmore. It is clipped to her obituary. He somberly hands the pair of documents to Samantha. She holds onto them long after she finishes reading. She had wanted to protect her friends, but now she supposed it didn't matter. Santos retrieves the documents, almost having to pry them from McCollum's fingers.

"We received a phone call," she says.

"We?"

"All five of us."

She hasn't spoken of this, ever. She had blocked it out and hasn't thought about it for years. Now it is being pried out of her, like the letter that Santos just removed from her hands, but it was stuck to her insides, hard and fast. Like creosote on the inside of her old stone chimney, it will have to be chiseled off, one layer at a time.

"He called us separately. We didn't know he was doing that."

Santos respects her silence, not interrupting.

"He offered me ten-thousand dollars. To say the nasty things about Mr. Whitmore. I told him, but they're not true. None of it is true. He said that Mr. Whitmore had abused the others and my testimony would corroborate theirs and would help put him behind bars where he belonged. I suppose that's what he told each of us."

"The money was the carrot," Santos says. "There must have been a stick. There always is. What was the stick?"

"If we refused, there would be a smear campaign. Word would get out that we were sluts, that we had encouraged Mr. Whitmore's advances. That we weren't virgins. That we drank. That we thought the words of our religious leaders were malarkey. None of it was true—"

"But none of it had to be, did it? People would believe it. Maybe not all, but some. You were all young and pretty. Personable Ballard Whitmore, recent BYU grad, was friendly with all of you. The rumors *could* be true. It's what people *could* think. The girls became too chummy. Whitmore wasn't the culprit. He was the *victim*! It was the girls who led him on. Into temptation. Your reputation would be tarnished one way or the other. Does that sound right?"

"Aye. And, he said that the rumors would land Mr. Whitmore in jail either way, so why not take the money and save yourself?"

"But you didn't! You didn't take the money! Why was that, Mrs. McCollum?"

"Please, don't ask me. I can't betray my friends!"

"They're no longer your friends. You haven't seen them for eleven years. They're all grown up, like you. They've gone their ways and you've gone yours. They've got husbands and children and homes, like you. They've got lives. Like you. Mr. Whitmore has not had a life for eleven years. He no longer has a wife or children or a home. His life came to a screeching halt for crimes he did not commit. Don't you think it's time you un-betrayed *him*?"

Thank God her children are at school. She wouldn't have been able to bear it with them here.

Again she looks at Whitmore, this time with tears in her eyes.

"Mr. Santos. It sounds so simple. I could not bring myself to lie like that."

"But your friends could? And did?"

"Evidently."

"Tell us the truth now, Mrs. McCollum. Who pressured you into doing all this? It is of the utmost importance if we're to see Mr. Whitmore exonerated."

"I don't know."

"You don't—"

"He never said his name. I swear it. I asked. He said it didn't matter, did it? And it didn't, because I didn't take the money and I didn't lie. Ask the other three. They'll tell you."

"We intend to, Mrs. McCollum. Now that we know some of the story. Is there anything else you can tell us?"

"What else is there?"

"The timing. Why all of a sudden, out of the blue, five of you get these threats to incriminate Mr. Whitmore? Why Mr. Whitmore? Why then?"

"I don't know! I don't know! I've always wondered why. I don't know. If you find out, please let me know. I mean that."

She looks at Whitmore. Is there sympathy for her in his eyes, or just disgust?

"Okay, Mrs. McCollum," Santos says. "We didn't want to trouble you when your children were here. We know this has been difficult."

"Thank you."

They stand up to leave. She isn't able to, and remains seated. She is shattered. Santos turns to Ballard Whitmore.

"Is there anything else?"

"Yes. I have a question. Two, actually."

"Yes?" Samantha asks.

"So you didn't take the money."

"That's right. I wanted to be honest."

"And you didn't accuse me, either. I suppose I should thank you for that."

"No need."

"Yet no one ever did spread any vicious rumors about *you*, did they? The rumors you and your friends were so worried about. You didn't suffer any consequences."

"I've thought about that. I suppose it's because they got what they wanted. Putting you in prison, I mean. But I was scared to death they'd hold it over me forever. That's why I left the country. I was scared."

"Too scared to tell the truth? You knew the truth all these years, yet you never spoke up. So my second question is, why are you any better than the rest of them? Think about that."

Whitmore and Santos walk down the lane back to the center of town and the Royal Arms B&B, where they had spent the previous night. It is only about a half mile, and it is a beautiful day, so they walk. Though summer is almost over, the walking warms them and Santos removes his jacket. As they approach the intersection with the main road where they will turn right to go into town, a car from their left makes a right turn and speeds into the lane, which is so narrow they have to back themselves up against the prickly hawthorn hedgerow to avoid getting run over.

The driver of the small, gray Peugeot hardly slows down for them, a driving tendency on Ireland's back lanes with which Whitmore and Santos have, in their short stay, already become familiar, but which cause them to wonder if all Irish are equally suicidal. They conclude the driver must have been Samantha McCollum's husband, Malcolm, anxious to return home from work, and are thankful they had conducted the interview, difficult as it was, without the added burden of his presence. They manage the rest of their walk without further threat to life and limb, and check out of their B&B. Before starting the long drive to the Dublin airport, Whitmore makes one phone call, to Phillip Valentine's fixer, Stewart Wolfe. He owes Valentine this courtesy. After all, how else would Whitmore have been able to afford their plane tickets?

Chapter Fifteen

Secretary of State Phillip Valentine, out of time and options, plays the last cards in his hand, but they might just as well have been aces and eights for the good it ends up doing him. His aide, Stewart Wolfe, again counseled against it, calling it political suicide. But Valentine has received a mild bump in the polls after taking his first swing implicating Layton Stolz in a sordid affair, so in desperation he forges ahead a second time, with the hope that lightning will strike twice and with fully lethal effect.

Wolfe has informed Valentine that Whitmore and Santos have made progress, good progress, in their effort to trace the origin of the sexual misconduct charges. They now know for sure there had been an extortion attempt, bribes paid, perjury committed. The bad news is that even though there is now a path forward, they still have no proof who was behind it. If they're lucky, the trail will lead all the back to Layton Stolz, or at least to his underlings. But there is no smoking gun, which infuriates Valentine. To him, it is so obvious. Hold your fire, Wolfe counsels.

Valentine disregards Wolfe and pulls the trigger. On national news, he publicly accuses Layton Stolz of being responsible for sending Ballard Whitmore, an innocent man, to prison for nine years by coercing certain individuals into making false charges. Valentine's difficulty is obvious. He has no evidence. Instead, he cites Whitmore's admirable character, his protestations of innocence, and the "eerie coincidence" of the allegations coming only two days after Whitmore, "one of our nation's finest music educators," publicly questioned the validity of Stolz's pet project, the Beethoven Sequence. He, Valentine, has knowledge, currently being investigated, that the false accusers accepted money to commit perjury in order to avoid having their good names besmirched. He insinuates the extortion effort was tied to the "Stolz machine," though again without any corroborating evidence. And though he knows damn sure the fact checkers will pounce on it within minutes, Valentine opts not to dilute his sound bite by mentioning that the charges for which Whitmore had been incarcerated involved sexual misconduct with minors.

As Wolfe had predicted, Valentine's Hail Mary backfired. Within hours, those members of the public who had forgotten about the Whitmore case, or who had never known about it in the first place, now know why Ballard Whitmore was sent to prison, leaving little sympathy for either him or Valentine, even if Valentine's wild allegations against Stolz held water. Questions are raised about Valentine's mental competence, let alone his ability to lead the country. There is a clamor for Layton Stolz to respond to the vile accusations. Though Stolz's inclination is to say nothing and let the situation play out on its own, at the urging of his staff he allowed Ann Smith to read a brief statement on his behalf.

"Mr. Stolz is deeply saddened his opponent would resort to taking the word of a sexual predator to try to influence the outcome of the election for president of the United States."

The next morning, Phillip Valentine's poll numbers hover just above the single digits.

"Things can't get any worse than this," he says.

"Let's hope not," Wolfe says, though he knows they are about to.

In late afternoon, Whitmore and Santos huddle at the investigator's office, sharing a Subway meatball footlong as they refine their message. They will contact the three surviving women—Kimberlea Heath, Joy Sparks, and Lexi Briscoe—whose false testimony had led to Whitmore's conviction, and notify them that as a result of unimpeachable information they have recently obtained, it was time for them to make a choice: Either come clean with us or we'll go to the authorities, who will charge you with perjury and accepting bribes, both of which, by the way, are felonies. If, on the other hand, you cooperate with us, nothing that will happen to you will compare to the suffering Ballard Whitmore has endured. Yes, we recognize that either choice will be painful for you, but look at how Ballard Whitmore's life has been turned upside down. In consideration for the difficulties cooperating with us will put you and your families through, we promise to be as discreet as possible, but one way or the other the truth will have to come out. It's up to you how it will.

At the conclusion of their meeting, Santos is wiping a bit of marinara sauce off his beard when there is a knock on the door. Santos opens the door a crack, keeping the chain on. There are two men. Whitmore, standing behind Santos, smiles when he sees them. They're clean cut and are wearing black suits and white shirts. Mormon missionaries! But after that first glance he revises his opinion. They're too old and excessively muscular to be your usual missionaries. They're also missing that innocent look and goofy smile, and aren't carrying a Book of Mormon. Observing the bulge under their coat jackets, he realizes they're not missionaries. At least not of the spiritual variety. The red-faced one with a bad complexion speaks first.

"Ballard Whitmore? Stavros Santos?"

"Yes. Why?"

"Federal marshals." They display their badges. "Come with us please. Both of you."

"Why?"

"We have a warrant for your arrests."

Both Whitmore and Santos are taken into custody and booked into the Salt Lake County metro jail. Whitmore and Santos are separated. The booking officer informs Whitmore that the embassy of the Republic of Ireland in Washington, D.C. has submitted a request to the U.S. State Department and the Office of International Affairs of the Criminal Division of the Department of Justice for his extradition. Whitmore is scheduled for a preliminary meeting with the extradition magistrate the next morning to review the charges against him and schedule a meeting for a formal hearing. Whitmore calls Richard Slyke before being escorted to a cell, where he spends a very long and very anxious night. The cell is clean and he isn't harassed.

But it's a cell, nevertheless. He doesn't know if he'll be able to endure it a second time around. Even for one night.

"Okay, explain to me what the heck is going on," Whitmore says to Slyke. It is 9:00 a.m. and the meeting with the judge is in a half hour.

"For some reason, Ballard, Ireland believes it has probable cause to extradite you to face criminal charges."

"For what?"

"We'll find out."

"And they can just lock me up?"

"For the time being, yes. Can I give you a short seminar in the extradition process? It's a little complicated."

"Go ahead. I don't have anything better to do at the moment."

"It's our executive branch that receives the initial request and makes the final decision, but the actual extradition proceedings are overseen by the judiciary. Basically, they make sure that all the details follow the letter of the law, and they'll make a recommendation."

"Executive branch. The president?"

"Not the president. The secretary of state, or more often someone in his department that he designates. But I'm jumping ahead. A warrant is sent from the Justice Department to a U.S. district court. They can authorize magistrate judges to preside over extradition requests. The proceedings usually start when the prosecuting attorney, say an Assistant U.S. Attorney, files the complaint indicating an intent to extradite. They usually seek what's called the provisional arrest of a fugitive if necessary to prevent the fugitive from fleeing before a formal extradition request is filed."

"But I'm not a fugitive."

"You and I know that, but we'll be finding out why they think you are, because the complaint includes information provided by the requesting country explaining why they think you should be extradited and why they think you're a flight risk. And the judge must have been convinced because she issued the warrant for your provisional arrest and Santos's."

"What happens now?"

"In a little while, you'll be brought before the judge for an initial appearance.

Sometimes the job is handed down to a local magistrate, but it looks like today it'll be Margaret Botford, who's the federal judge for the Utah District. So reading the tea leaves, it looks like this is no ordinary case."

"What do you know about this Botford?"

"She's been around the block and knows the law inside out. The tough-but-fair type. Not much meat on her bones, so people think she'll be a pushover, but she's got a steel backbone. I'd counsel keeping everything upfront."

"How do we know what upfront means when we don't even know what I'm here for?"

"That's what this preliminary meeting is about. She'll inform you that extradition is being sought by Ireland to answer some specific charges, and the sentence which it would carry. You'll be advised of your rights and they'll consider bail pending the extradition hearing."

"This isn't the hearing?"

"No. This is just the initial appearance. Botford will explain things, like making sure we understand that this is not a trial. They don't determine guilt or innocence here. They just decide whether there's enough evidence to recommend extradition. Then she'll set a date for the government to advise us of the evidence it plans to introduce at the extradition hearing, like the names of witnesses and expected scope of their testimony. They'll also give us copies of documents it intends to introduce. She'll schedule a reciprocal date for us to do the same. Then she'll schedule a firm hearing date."

"Will I have to stay in jail until then?"

"Probably. They hardly ever grant bail in extraditions. Countries take their international obligations seriously, so when one requests extradition, the other usually tries to be accommodating. Part of the bigger picture of international relations. You'd have to be really, really ill to get bail, or have some other serious mitigating circumstance. And with your criminal record, I doubt you'd get it."

"So how long are we talking before the hearing? A week? Two? I've already spent nine years in jail for something I didn't do. I can't handle going back for a crime I don't even know about yet."

"The good news is that we can get a bail ruling very quickly."

"And the bad news?"

"It can take up to a year or more to get the hearing. Fortunately, you're not a fugitive. If you were on the lam, it could be years."

A year! He had already lost almost a third of his life, and now he might have to wait a year just to find out if he was going to be sent to another country to be put on trial for a crime he had no idea about. Whitmore told himself to breathe, which he realized he had stopped doing.

"I can't do it, Richard. I can't go back to jail for a year waiting for a hearing. And for what? What have I done?"

"There is one way to speed it up."

"What's that?"

"You can waive the hearing and consent to be extradited. You'd go to Ireland, stand trial, and hopefully be acquitted. You say you haven't done anything. That might be the easiest way out."

"But you say they have probable cause."

"Yeah. They think there's a good chance you and/or Santos will be convicted. Otherwise, they probably wouldn't have gone to all this trouble. Extradition is not an everyday affair."

"Isn't there any other way to get out of this than agreeing to be extradited?"

"We can always try habeas corpus."

"What's that?"

"We could challenge the constitutionality of the whole proceeding. Fight the extradition. Claim your rights have been unfairly violated. Find a loophole in the treaty between Ireland and Washington. It's been done."

"Would I still have to stay in jail?"

"Yes."

"Would it still take a year?"

"More or less. The longer we fight it, of course, the longer you'll be in jail."

"What are the chances of winning?"

"Depends on whether all the i's have been dotted, and maybe what the charges are. But, to be totally honest, the chances are not very good."

Whitmore and Slyke are led into the chambers of Justice Margaret Botford.

She seems curiously out of place with the lawyerly, heavy decor of the room, not unlike Slyke's office. A slight woman in her late sixties, she appears to have little regard for personal appearance, wearing no makeup; and any attention she might have paid to her unkempt mass of graying hair was clearly in the distant past. Yet there is something quite powerful in those eyes behind the thick glasses, clearly intimating that BS is not going to be tolerated in her chambers. On the bookshelf behind her are some small, framed photos. Children? Grandchildren? Loved ones, quite possibly. Too far away to tell, but Whitmore hopes it is a sign of empathy, of good things to come. Sitting at her elevated bench, Botford wishes Whitmore and Slyke good morning and gestures for them to take a seat opposite her.

She first asks to see Whitmore's driver's license to confirm his identity. As she inspects it, Slyke said, "I'm Richard Slyke, and I'm representing—"

"Yes, I know who you are." Botford says. "Your reputation as an ambulance chaser precedes you, and if I need information I'll ask for it, thank you."

Satisfied with the results of the ID, she hands the license back to Whitmore.

She continues, "I have here a duly authorized and signed Certification of Extraditability and Order of Commitment for the extradition of Ballard Whitmore to the Republic of Ireland. All the paperwork seems to be in order."

She hands a copy to Slyke.

"May I ask the charge, please?" Whitmore says.

"The charge is first-degree murder, Mr. Whitmore."

Slyke tries unsuccessfully to restrain Whitmore from jumping out of his chair.

"That's impossible!" Whitmore shouts. "This is a setup. I didn't kill anybody!"

"When you're finished ranting, Mr. Whitmore," Botford says, "I'll provide you with the nature of and the basis for the underlying criminal charges, which is what led me to issue the warrant for your provisional arrest. Now please take your counsel's advice and sit down or you will only make the situation worse for yourself than it already is, if that's possible.

"Let me remind you that you will have your day in court to respond to the charges. However, today is not that day. Today is the day you'll listen, and only listen. Is that understood?"

Whitmore nods, and sits back down. He would have even if he hadn't been ordered to, because he is in shock and his legs cannot support him.

"Two days ago," Botford continues, "a woman, Samantha McCollum, living in Kilcrohane, County Cork, Ireland, was discovered dead by her two small children returning home from school. Mrs. McCollum had been gagged and bound to a chair. Her skull had been fractured from a blow to the back of the head, presumably by a heavy iron teapot found next to the body. It had skull fragments on it. Pardon me for editorializing, but one can only imagine what the moment of finding their mother murdered must have been like for the children. The children called the father, who immediately returned home and then called the police. The children, when they were able to speak, described two men they encountered on their way to school. Their description matched you and Mr. Santos. The bed and breakfast in the town there provided your identification. As far as anyone can tell, you and Mr. Santos were the last people to see Mrs. McCollum alive. Their medical examiner places her time of death approximately a half hour before you arrived back at the bed and breakfast to check out. The Irish authorities believe there is sufficient evidence for you to be surrendered to their justice system, and I tend to concur. However, attorney Slyke has perhaps made you aware that I'm not the decider in this case. I only recommend. The State Department makes the final determination. We will schedule a hearing with the Assistant United States Attorney at a time that is mutually convenient. Until then, you'll remain in custody of the state."

"Your Honor," Slyke said. "We would like to request bail for Mr. Whitmore. Mr. Whitmore is working a full-time job and is not a flight risk. He'll be happy to accommodate any requirements the court may impose to verify his whereabouts."

"Like an ankle bracelet?"

"Yes, like an ankle bracelet."

Botford appears to give the request some thought, tapping her fingers on her desk for a few seconds.

"Considering the serious nature of the charges, and considering that Mr. Whitmore already has a criminal record, I'm going to deny bail. Are there any more questions?"

There is a knock on the door. An elderly uniformed man enters. Whitmore assumes it is the bailiff who will lead him away, but instead the man approaches Justice Botford and speaks quietly into her ear.

"Excuse me a moment," she says to Whitmore and Slyke. She and the man leave the chambers.

It is more than a moment. The moment becomes minutes, and the minutes more than a half hour, when Botford returns. Whatever she has been told, she belies nothing in her demeanor or in the tone of her voice.

"Mr. Whitmore," she says. "It seems you have a guardian angel. I've been informed that you are to be released and your hearing has been put on hold indefinitely. You are free to go. For now."

"For now?"

"Yes, because you are to keep your nose clean, and if you so much as sneeze in the wrong direction, I'll have you thrown back into a cell. At my insistence, you are to surrender your passport and remain in the state. Enjoy your liberty, Mr. Whitmore, because who knows how long it will last."

"May I ask," asked Slyke, "who Mr. Whitmore's guardian angel is?"

"You may ask," Botford replies, "but you're not going to get an answer, at least from me. Good day."

It is unseasonably warm outside the courthouse, warmer even than it had been inside. If not for a cooling northwesterly breeze that blew in a bit of the salty brine from the Great Salt Lake, the early October morning would have felt like midsummer. Whitmore's phone rings, and after a brief exchange, his dazed euphoria is replaced by a somber reality.

"What was that about?" Slyke asks.

"Looks like I'm screwed either way," he says.

"What do you mean?"

"After the election, one or the other of them, Valentine or Stolz, will use me as cannon fodder."

"This is all news to me, friend. Care to fill me in?"

"I'm a liability to Phillip Valentine. He wanted me to get incriminating information on Stolz, which led us to Samantha McCollum, but the only thing I delivered was a murdered woman. And like the judge said, can you imagine those kids finding their mother bludgeoned to death? As far as the world will view it, I'm not just a pedophile. I'm a murdering pedophile. For now, Stewart Wolfe just wants me to shut up about the trip to Ireland, but if Valentine wins the election next month, he'll reissue the extradition order and I'll be dead meat."

"What does Stewart Wolfe have to do with this?"

"He's the one who just called me. A friendly reminder that it was due to pressure from Phillip Valentine that the request for my extradition was deep-sixed, but Wolfe threatened me that they'll resurrect it if I don't keep my mouth shut. 'Just remember who your friends are,' quote unquote."

"But why Wolfe?"

"Wolfe paid for the plane tickets for Santos and me to go to Ireland."

"And how do you see Layton Stolz fitting into this?"

"With Stolz it's even worse, if you can imagine that. I know it was Stolz who was behind forcing those girls to put me in prison, and I know he was behind Samantha McCollum's murder, so he has even more to lose than Valentine."

"We don't know those things for sure."

"It was Stolz," Whitmore said. "Valentine had no reason to kill her and every reason to keep her alive. Stolz had every reason see her disappear. And we led him to her. I know it was him."

The key, they agreed, was the man in the gray Peugeot that had driven by them on the way to the house in Kilcrohane. Whitmore and Santos had assumed it was the husband, but if what the children said is correct, he must have been the killer. If they could identify the driver, they could tie it all back to Stolz.

"Will Santos tell the authorities the same story you're telling me?" Slyke asks.

"Do you mean can we trust him, or that you think I'm lying?"

"Neither. But if you both have the same story, related independently, it at least corroborates what you've been saying, which is that you're innocent and they need to find a man in a Peugeot. Did either of you have a good view of the driver?"

"No, neither of us. The car went by too quickly. We had to dive into a hedge, so identifying the driver was the last thing on our minds. But it was a man."

"A car going in the general direction of the house, with an unidentifiable driver. That's not going to cut the mustard. Is there some way to demonstrate you were on a quest for information and not on a trail of revenge? Because I'm sorry to say that's what it looks like."

"Call Stewart Wolfe," Whitmore says, with a bitter laugh.

"You know what?" Slyke said. "This reminds me of a case I had last winter. Person X, my client, was skiing down a slope up at Snowbird. He skied into Person Y, who was just standing there, who sued my client for injuries. We turned around and sued the pants off him for recklessly being in the way."

"What's your point?"

"Turning the tables. If Wolfe used a credit card, we might have the connection to get you off the hook. You'd have him over a barrel. They'd have to keep protecting you."

"I wish. But Wolfe paid cash. He wanted to maintain his distance. That was fine with me at the time. There was no other way I could get to Ireland, so I didn't argue. And we do have an enemy in common. Layton Stolz."

Slyke does call Stewart Wolfe. Many times. He wants to get Wolfe to say, one way or another, that he helped his client, Ballard Whitmore, go to Ireland to interview Samantha McCollum. Not to kill her. Just to talk to her. One of Wolfe's aides eventually calls back, with an unambiguous answer: Mr. Wolfe has no knowledge whatsoever of a trip Mr. Whitmore took to Ireland. Yes, he had given Mr. Whitmore the benefit of the doubt in regard to his protestations of innocence over his conviction for sexual misconduct, but now that it appears Mr. Whitmore is a murderer as well as a sexual deviant, Mr. Wolfe realizes he had been deceived by Mr. Whitmore. Any further attempts by Mr. Whitmore to communicate with the Secretary will immediately be referred to the Department of Justice.

"Was it absolutely necessary to kill an innocent woman?" Ann Smith asks. She is appalled at the news. Over the phone, Sheely's voice is as taut as a stretched steel wire.

"An innocent *man* would have been okay?" he responds.

"You know what I mean."

"It's none of your business. You don't want to know."

"I need to know."

"If you must. It was not only necessary. It's driven the final nail in Valentine's coffin."

And the final nail in Whitmore's also, Sheely thought.

"Collect the music," Ann Smith ordered Duane, who has just put his viola back in its case. It is at the end of a Saturday morning rehearsal at Flora High. He has balked. He has been doing all the work lately, while behind his back she has been building a wall between him and Mr. Stolz, one brick at a time. Like she owns him.

"Collect it yourself," he says.

Ann Smith looks at him with that superior look. Just because he's a high school student and she's at least twice his age. Still, fair is fair. Why should she be doing all the ordering and he all the obeying?

Ann Smith doesn't say a word, but instead goes into the room with the soundproof door Mr. Stolz uses as an office. She is talking to Mr. Stolz. Duane can't hear a word, but as he gathers the folders from the music stands, he glances sideward to see what is happening. She is standing in front of Mr. Stolz. He is sitting down, looking up at her, a look of bewilderment—or is it a frown—on his face. Duane can tell she's angry because she doesn't move a muscle as she talks. That's how she always gets when she doesn't like something. Stiff. She leaves the office, ignoring him. Duane pretends not to notice. With the door open, Mr. Stolz calls to him.

"Duane, can you come in here a moment, please?"

He puts the pile of folders he's collected next to the door and goes in.

Until Mr. Stolz started the Sequence program, Duane was bullied in school on a daily basis. Pushed around, insulted, taunted, and worse. His foster parents—the word "parents," when applied to them was a joke—were uninterested at best. They were more concerned getting their monthly government check. But Mr. Stolz brought respect, and over time the school beatings stopped. It was a miracle. Duane no longer contemplated suicide. Well, not as often, anyway. He would die for Layton Stolz. But he would not die for Ann Smith.

"Duane, I've appreciated the work you've done for me," Stolz says. "It goes far beyond how well you've done just playing in the orchestra, which in itself is all that I could ever have asked for."

But? Duane thinks. He knows there's a "but" that's going to come. He can hear it in Mr. Stolz's voice. Is he going to make him apologize to Ann Smith? He will if he has to. Is he going to be kicked out of the orchestra? That's the worst possibility he can imagine. He waits for the verdict.

There's silence. It's almost as if Mr. Stolz wants him to ask, but Duane can't come up with the right words. They both wait, looking at each other, trying to fathom each other's thoughts.

"Duane, I think it would be a good idea for you to have a mentor on a daily basis. Someone you can look up to. Someone who could be your role model. A friend, even."

Duane is relieved. This is the best of all outcomes. "That would be you," Duane says. "Right?"

Stolz seems to be taken aback. What else could he have meant? Duane wonders.

"Well, I'm honored you should think that," Stolz says. "But I had someone else in mind. Someone closer to your own age."

Duane thinks, but has no idea.

"Who?" he asks.

"I'm thinking of that young man, Ballard Whitmore."

"Ballard?"

"Yes, he's a fine, well-behaved young man, always with something positive to say. Always with a smile. Not to mention he plays the violin very, very well. Maybe you could even play duets together."

Duane is dizzy. He wants to throw up. He tastes the bile, but holds it back. "A fine young man." No one had ever called him "a fine young man." Until this moment, Duane had never understood the motivation of the bullies who punched him in the stomach and tripped him in the hallways, who pulled his pants down in the locker room. But now he does. It would feel so good to kill Ballard Whitmore.

"Whatever you say," Duane says.

"I'm so glad you agree," Stolz says. There is relief in his voice.

For four months, until Ballard Whitmore leaves for his mission, Duane Sheely pretends.

"I don't approve of your blood lust, Duane," Ann Smith says.

"I couldn't care less what you approve or disapprove of."

"Just make sure no one connects the dots to Layton."

"Dots? There are no dots."

Chapter Sixteen

It is an inauguration unlike any other. As tradition dictates, the Chief Justice of the Supreme Court first delivers the oath of office to the new Vice President of the United States, Duane Sheely. Next is the main event, the swearing in of President Layton Stolz. After solemnly pledging to faithfully execute the office of President of the United States and, to the best of his ability, preserve, protect, and defend the Constitution of the United States, Layton Stolz commences his inauguration speech with the same words he addressed the school board of Flora, Colorado with many years before: "How many of you know the *Egmont Overture*?" On this occasion, however, on a sunny, blustery day in January, a deafening roar rises like a tidal wave from the vast sea of dedicated followers from every corner of the nation, gathered together on the National Mall for the historic moment. Media would later report that the Secret Service estimated it might have been the largest public gathering in the history of the United States, even greater than the estimated throng of five million that celebrated the Chicago Cubs' victory in the 2016 World Series.

The election results were a foregone conclusion. It had been the second-biggest electoral landslide of all time, behind only Franklin Roosevelt's 1936 trouncing of Alf Landon. Favorite son Phillip Valentine had taken New York by a hair. Stolz won the other forty-nine states. Phillip Valentine had received nineteen percent of the popular vote, Vincent Lancaster a mere ten percent, and Stolz, as a write-in candidate, had received sixty-eight percent, easily beating the previous record of sixty-one percent set by Lyndon Johnson against Barry Goldwater in 1964.

In his inauguration speech, Stolz extols the achievements of the Beethoven Sequence, made possible only by the tireless work and determination of so many within and without the BSA organization, many of whom will assuredly find places in his new administration. He thanks the hundreds-of-thousands of students and former students, whose dedication over the years of the program has resulted in returning America to its exalted position of being the beacon of the world in so many ways. He promises that the best is yet to come, that a new dawn of heretofore unimaginable American transcendence will soon be realized.

Stolz's inauguration speech is the shortest in American history, less than ten minutes long, partly because Layton Stolz, like Abraham Lincoln, is a man of few words and uncomfortable in the public spotlight. His voice lacks sonority and nuance. Rather, it is straightforward and, if one were to be critical, dull. Also, the speech is short because it is merely a prelude to the grand event that is to come. For instead of the whirl of ostentatious, expensive inaugural balls for the hoity-toity, where a tango of business deals, ambassadorships, and political favors traditionally find promising dancing partners, Stolz has planned something brazenly audacious and something far more meaningful to him personally. Drawing inspiration from conductor Leonard Bernstein and the fall of the Berlin Wall, it will be something with which he intends to illuminate the souls of rich and poor, weak and powerful, circling the entire globe. That night, inauguration night, at the concert hall of the John F. Kennedy Center for the Performing Arts in Washington, D.C., the National Symphony Orchestra will perform Beethoven's Ninth Symphony, broadcast nationally on every radio and television network. The conductor will be Layton Stolz, president of the United States.

Brash? Unorthodox? Revolutionary? That's what they've said about me, Layton Stolz thinks. That's how they've defined me. But unprecedented? Yes and no. Wasn't it true that Thomas Jefferson was also a serious, well-schooled musician? A violinist who practiced three hours a day for years? Didn't he declare that music "is the favorite passion of my soul"? And wasn't Benjamin Franklin an enlightened amateur musician who played three different instruments, invented the glass harmonica, and composed music? And didn't John F. Kennedy, while not a musician himself, champion the arts, welcoming the greatest musicians to perform in the White House?

It will be the moment of validation Stolz has been waiting for all these years. Invited to the concert are dignitaries from around the globe and luminaries of the classical music world like Yo-Yo Ma and Itzhak Perlman. Five hundred seats were reserved for Stolz's loyal Sequence instructors. He made sure to reserve one other for the dean of admissions of the Juilliard School of Music. The last seat in the top balcony.

Stolz is undeterred that in all his years conducting his Beethoven Sequence—the *Egmont Overture*, three symphonies, the four *Leonora* overtures—he has never conducted an orchestra of professional musicians. He has honed his technique with students, and with them the results have become predictably inspirational. The students, starting with music totally alien to them, worked tirelessly to perfect the music. Now he will be working with musicians who do it for a living, who already know the music. It should be that much easier. He is well aware that many of the musicians, particularly those from overseas in Europe and Asia, have not been trained in his particular, idiosyncratic method. Nevertheless, they are professionals, highly paid ones at that, and though there would only be two rehearsals, not the thirty-odd he is accustomed to, Stolz is confident that, given their experience, he will be able to communicate his interpretation with little difficulty.

So he is a bit confounded when the first rehearsal, held two days before the inauguration, gets off to a rocky start. The orchestra is perplexingly out of kilter. The balances are off. At times, the primary instruments are barely audible. It is rhythmically choppy, lacking a natural flow. Entrances are inaccurate and tempos fluctuate listlessly. The way things are going, he will need much more time than the two-and-a-half-hour rehearsal the contract allows. By the time the musicians take their break an hour-and-fifteen-minutes in, a sense of unease, if not dissension, is palpable. Stolz has long progressed beyond Müller's book, *How to Conduct*, but now he is beginning to wish he had paid more than scant attention to *Chapter Ten: Working with Professionals*, which he had more or less ignored, since the situation had never arisen.

The orchestra vacates the stage for twenty minutes of coffee and gossip in the lounge. Stolz, mystified, sits in an empty chair in the cello section. He hasn't felt this helpless since the first time he conducted the F-natural to begin the *Egmont Overture*.

Stephen Kim, concertmaster of the orchestra for twelve years, approaches Stolz on the quiet stage, his violin under his arm. His attitude is benevolent.

"Excuse me," he says. "I'm not sure what to call you, sir. Maestro? Mister President Elect?"

"Mr. Stolz will be fine. I don't understand the problem here. No one seems to be following me."

"If I may be so bold, Mr. Stolz. The problem is that we're professionals. We've played Beethoven Nine a hundred times, and you're conducting us like—well, to be blunt—like we're students. Like we've never heard this before. May I say, like you're trying to teach the alphabet to Shakespeare."

"But that's the only way I know how. I've memorized every note, every gesture."

"And you can be sure we appreciate that and all you've done for music education. But may I be frank?"

"Go on."

"If you want a good performance, and I assume you do because the whole world is going to be our audience, all you need to do—the best thing you can do—is just sit back, stay out of the way, and follow the orchestra. We know how it goes. We know how to make it sound good. And we know how to make a conductor look good. We do it all the time."

"But what about the passion?"

"The passion's in the music, Mr. Stolz. Beethoven put it there. The passion's in the music, and in the occasion. Don't you worry."

"I'll think about it. Where did you say you studied?" Stolz asked.

"I didn't. But it was Juilliard."

"I see. Thank you very much, Mr. Kim."

On the night of the concert, the packed Kennedy Center concert hall is electric with anticipation. The performance of the Ninth Symphony, carrying its message of freedom and brotherhood, reverberates around the world. The passion, intensified by the historic nature of the moment, is as overwhelming as it is inevitable. It comes through in the musicians' playing and in the chorus' and vocal soloists' singing. The audience hears it, feels it, and responds to it. Bravos echo for a half hour after the final chord of a performance deemed "supernally inspirational" by *The Washington Post* the next morning. America's claim of moral leadership among the community of nations has been reasserted without a shot being fired or a dollar being spent. Layton Stolz is a hero yet again.

After the concert, the musicians pack their instruments and change into street clothes. Stephen Kim, the concertmaster, is heading out the Kennedy Center artists' entrance, anxious to go home and have a glass of sherry with his wife before going to bed. The orchestra has a rehearsal for next week's program in the morning.

"Message for you, Mr. Kim," the guard says. "President's chief of staff says to wait here. She'll be here in a minute."

Kim calls home and tells his wife he'll be delayed. He doesn't know how long. Kiss the kids for me.

Whether Ann Smith had intentionally waited until all the other musicians departed was unknowable, but she arrives the moment Kim is the only musician left.

"I understand you had a conversation with President Stolz at the rehearsal," she says. "About his conducting."

"I gave him a few pointers, yes," Kim replies. "I hope they were helpful."

"Just make sure you don't mention your little chat with the president to anyone. Ever."

"Is that message from him or from you?"

"One doesn't ask questions like that. You should remember that."

"Well, it doesn't really matter anyway."

"Why not?"

"Because even without me saying a word, everyone in the orchestra knew the truth after the first five minutes of the first rehearsal. And in the orchestra world, word gets around."

The next morning, with the welcome freshness of early spring already in the air, Layton Stolz issues an executive order in a Rose Garden ceremony, his first official act as President of the United States. Ann Smith hands him the document, which he signs with his modest, careful signature, formally codifying the concept of liberty through music. The order mandates that every public school embark upon a Sequence music program to the exclusion of any other. For such an extensive project, Stolz will handpick a committee to write a new textbook for all music teachers to follow, integrating the great musical tradition of Western Europe with American cultural history, philosophy, literature, and the sciences. Stolz promises that American education, having regained its world preeminence as a result of the Sequence, will become the template for all other countries to follow.

In the past, the costs of Sequence programs had been borne by generous donors. But in order to pay for this monumental expansion, he proposes an additional one percent income tax on the wealthy to be devoted solely to the new program. He expects the legislation will pass with little opposition from Congress, as its membership—and likewise in state and local governments—now includes a growing number of Sequence disciples. He is confident that once enacted, local school boards will welcome the federal government's partnership—not intrusion, as some critics might be inclined to say—in the formulation of the curriculum, having been relieved of the burden of the cost.

The Cheshire Cat smiles of officials standing behind Stolz as he signs his first executive order suggest they are totally committed to his vision. They have little choice. The gathered press, on the other hand, rumble. "Mister President!" "Mister President!"

President Stolz raises his hand to quell the ruckus. He assures the members of the media that he understands their legitimate concerns—yes, he knows all about government overreach—and asks for their patience. Wait and see. Don't judge too soon. Let's see what happens. I think you'll agree, like everyone else, it's for the good of our country.

After the press and his staff have dispersed from the signing ceremony, President Stolz and Ann Smith return to the Oval Office.

"Ann, please put me on the phone with Dignan."

Stolz calmly explains to Alan Dignan, managing director of the National Symphony, that upon reflection he feels it isn't entirely appropriate for the concertmaster of the nation's bellwether orchestra to be a foreigner. Perhaps another position could be found for Kim or maybe he should even be sent back to his homeland in Korea, where his talents might be more appreciated.

Dignan politely explains why it is impossible to do that. First of all, the NSO musicians and the organization are legally bound by a union-sanctioned collective bargaining agreement. There are very specific rules and regulations for non-renewal or re-seating of musicians, and nothing in the CBA permits acceding to a request like the one Stolz is making. Second, Stephen Kim is Korean American, born and raised in New York City. He is as American as Abraham Lincoln.

Nevertheless, something really needs to be done, Stolz perseveres. One would not want to jeopardize millions of dollars of funding for the orchestra over a simple misunderstanding. Might not the contract have a provision for dismissal for cause? Most contracts do. Bad behavior, sexual harassment, that sort of thing.

Yes, but.

Does Dignan really need more guidance than that? Does it have to be spelled out? Perhaps it would be clearer to a different managing director.

Understood.

I knew I could count on you.

Chapter Seventeen

After much persuasion, she convinces Whitmore to meet her. He proposes Denny's on South State. Why Denny's? The food there is cheap and edible enough, the snow is coming down, and it's a block from the Sunset View Motel, and he doesn't own a hat or a winter coat.

Sandy Duckworthy, now a senior writer for the *Flora Daily Ledger*, has maintained her fascination with the Layton Stolz saga since the very beginning. Her *Stolz, Layton* file had long ago become an entire file cabinet, then two. No other story, even fiction, compared to the Stolz story. To rise from an unknown, small-town metalworker to become a cult-like Pied Piper of classical music, and then to ascend to the presidency of the United States! And now, Ballard Whitmore, convicted child molester, has become part of the thread. She was intrigued to read the news of Whitmore's on-again, off-again extradition, which had been reported in the major papers. Upon the advice of counsel, Whitmore had kept a low profile, not granting interviews. The private investigator, Stavros Santos, had also maintained his silence, even from Whitmore, or so it was reported. As a result, the going theory, unrefuted by anyone, was that Whitmore had hired Santos to help him track down Samantha McCollum in order to kill her. The big question being asked was why. Why did Whitmore kill her? No one had come up with a particularly convincing narrative, but, with his past history as a sex offender and the abundance of circumstantial evidence, there was little doubt that one would soon emerge.

They're sitting in a booth in the back of Denny's, away from prying eyes. Whitmore looks across the table directly at Duckworthy. She is dressed conservatively, in a long dress and button-down sweater, though somehow she radiates a sensuality that he has to concentrate on overlooking.

"How did you get my number?" he asks. First, Layton Stolz had wanted his address. Then, the Acura had followed him and Santos to southern Utah. Since then, Whitmore has been looking over his shoulder wherever he goes, daily changing his route between his motel and workplace. Now, this reporter from out of the blue wants to talk to him, and she'd gotten his phone number. Why should he trust her more than anyone else? Short answer, he doesn't.

"I'm an investigative journalist. When I get my teeth into a story, I find the ways. It wasn't easy. That's all I can tell you."

"What do you want?"

"To hear your side of the story."

"Why?"

"I'll answer your question if you let me ask one."

"I'm not interested in helping you sell newspapers."

"And I'm not interested in reading the same fairy tales about why you allegedly killed Samantha McCollum."

"Okay. Ask a question."

"Thank you. Let me give you a little background." She has prepared her pitch. "Except for his inner circle, I know as much about the mind of Layton Stolz as anyone," she says. "At first I was one of his cheerleaders. Music, education, freedom, the whole ball of wax. Back when it all started, when he gave Phillip Valentine and the feds a black eye back in Flora, I was rah-rah along with everyone else. People power. A feel-good story. It helped make us small town yokels feel important when there wasn't much else that did. Then, a few years later, Duane Sheely pulled the same stunt in Smirewood, knocking Sheffield Harrington out of the running at the Iowa caucuses. That's when I started having reservations. You see, the first time, with Stolz, it was an accident. A happy coincidence. The second time it was intentional. It was intimidation. And it's been getting worse ever since. You know, 'slamming a Beethoven.' That's what they've called it for years. And with pride."

"So?"

"So, when you first were accused of the sex charges, everyone figured you were just one more teacher who couldn't keep it in his pants. Who betrayed the trust of his students. There was no reason at all for anyone to believe it was anything other than that. But you talked about the timing. In fact, you wouldn't shut up about it. That the hammer dropped two days after you'd dared to question the wisdom of Layton Stolz. The more I thought about it, the more it seemed possible it was a variation on a growing theme, no double entendre intended. I put your case in the Stolz file, and there it stayed until your recent release and even more recent re-arrest."

"And now? What is it you want? You writing a book? You need my permission for the movie rights?"

"I want what you want, Ballard! I want to find out the truth about Layton Stolz. And if it is indeed Layton Stolz behind all this, to nail him. Now, will you let me ask a question for a change? After all, I'm here to interview you, not the other way around."

"Go ahead."

"Okay, I'll make it simple. Will you stop being a dumbass and tell me everything you know?"

Whitmore never has taken to coffee. His religion doesn't permit it, and, even though he is no longer a member, he tried it once and can't stand the taste. Mountain Dew has become his stimulant of choice. Denny's offers free refills, which turns out to be a good thing, because he makes an instinctive decision. Time to stop being paranoid and start trusting someone. He has to if he is going to stay sane. If he's going to tell his story to Duckworthy, he figures they'll be there for a long time. He'll need those free refills.

Two hours later, on their way out, Duckworthy asks Whitmore, "Know any places to stay here in town? It was a nine-hour drive from Flora, and I don't relish the thought of driving another five hundred miles home."

"You could share my room," he offers.

Duckworthy raises an eyebrow. Whitmore can't believe what he just said. The catharsis of opening up to someone—and someone as attractive as Duckworthy—did more wonders than he had imagined possible, but he fears he has gone too far.

"But it's got bedbugs," he finishes, retreating to safer ground.

Duckworthy looks into his eyes. Whitmore looks back. He thinks maybe she likes him for some reason. Maybe because she tended to believe his story, now that she understands it fully. Maybe because she sympathizes with his situation.

"An invitation like that's tough to pass up, handsome, but I think I'll splurge on a Motel 6," she says.

Whitmore looks downcast.

"For now, anyway," she says. "Smile."

Through his own long experience with the Sequence, Layton Stolz understands the vital importance of disciplined execution of a plan. Teamwork is essential. Trust. Loyalty. Pride in the product. Pride in the achievement. Inspiring young people. Building confidence. But it always comes back to discipline. Discipline is the key. That is one reason why, as president, he has appointed Arlene Covington, former director of music programs in Dubuque, Iowa, vice-president of National School Music Educators Association, and BSA Mideastern Regional Director, to become his Secretary of Education. Covington knows the BSA system and she knows music, a winning combination.

It was her masterful execution of Stolz's most recent brainstorm that has made BSA more powerful than ever. In addition to the traditional Saturday morning weekly Beethoven rehearsals, there are now Monday evening "getting together" meetings with the parents. Each meeting begins with one or more parents testifying how Beethoven and Layton Stolz have changed their lives. Though testimony is strictly voluntary, the chapter heads carefully record the names of those who have stood up and those who haven't. As a result, most parents feel the spirit move them to testify sooner or later. Sometimes the entire meeting time is taken up by enthusiastic parents joyfully recounting how their children's lives have been uplifted by the *Eroica* Symphony or by President Stolz's most recent proclamation about freedom. In whatever time remains, chapter heads announce the activities for the week and assign the parents and their children specific tasks. The activities extend beyond practicing and performing the music—though those endeavors remain the core, of course—and may include things like potluck Beethoven bashes or going from door to door to talk to neighbors about how they, too, might pitch in to make America even stronger. Individual assignments are duly noted on a bulletin board for all to see and are conspicuously checked off as they are accomplished. One does not want to be the last person checked off.

As a tough administrator, Covington also knows how to keep maverick teachers in line. If someone strays from the straight and narrow, it is at their own peril. First, there is a warning: Don't mess with success. If you do, you're compromising your funding and therefore the success of your students. You wouldn't want to do that, would you? If the message still goes unheeded, there is the nuclear option, which Stolz finds very distasteful, but sometimes there is no alternative. Terminating the teacher, which means terminating his or her employment, of course. Covington is a pro at that, but, after a few highly public whippings, she found it was hardly necessary.

Likewise, when from time to time President Stolz encountered resistance to his ideas about the economy or international affairs, which happens less and less, the most effective remedy was to investigate, then arrest the offender. It is a powerful deterrent. And the more highly positioned the offender, the better the deterrent to others. That's why he encouraged—of course, he couldn't order—the FBI to arrest former Secretary of State and presidential candidate Phillip Valentine. They had reported to him that Valentine, through his fixer, Stewart Wolfe, had provided the funding for Ballard Whitmore and Stavros Santos to go to Ireland to confront Samantha McCollum. Bad judgement on Valentine's part, because now it will be inevitable that the public will tie him to the McCollum murder. How the mighty fall through their own rash behavior. Vice President Sheely will leak bits of information to the media—just accurate enough to provide a cover of plausible deniability—about the Wolfe-Whitmore connection. The innuendo will be enough to convince the public. And it will be as much as the public will get. It's just a shame that Ballard will be a casualty in all of this. Such a promising lad. Oh, well. Friendly fire. Sometimes there's no avoiding it. The greater good. Once they find him.

Stolz's vision is Beethoven's offspring: to create a society in which men are free and equal. If someone opposes his plans, then they must by definition be against freedom and equality. In the end, there is no opposition. Everyone sees things Layton Stolz's way. Ergo, everyone is free.

Sandy Duckworthy calls the next afternoon.

"Ready for another Mountain Dew, Ballard?" she asks.

The snow has stopped, cleansing the air. Though the sky is a brilliant, crystalline azure, the temperature has plummeted and the sidewalks have turned to ice.

"Can't we do this over the phone?"

"Better in person. I don't trust the phones. I'll explain. Fifteen minutes?"

"Okay."

They find the same corner booth.

"Are you sure you don't want some coffee?" Duckworthy asks. "Blue lips don't become you."

Whitmore is too cold to imagine her with no clothes on.

"It was your idea to meet, not mine," he said. "What's so important?"

"Something fishy's been going on."

"That's an understatement," Whitmore replies.

"I've tried contacting the three women. Heath, Briscoe, and Sparks. To corroborate your side of the story. Are you sure you haven't contacted them?"

"I already told you that yesterday."

"Don't get testy, Ballard. I just need to confirm it because of what's been going on."

"Yes. I'm sure," Whitmore said. "Santos and I were arrested before we could send them our offer, and since then we've had to stay away from them or we'd get rearrested. I'm sure of that, too."

"Okay. So this is what's up. I called each one of them, and, as soon as I identified myself as a reporter, they hung up. Immediately. So I took an Uber to their addresses and knocked on their doors. No response, even though there were lights on, cars in the garage, and I could smell food cooking in the Briscoe house. Then I emailed them. No response. I followed it up with another email, and I got that Mailer-Daemon shit—pardon my French—indicating those addresses were permanently deleted even though the previous emails had gone through no problem an hour before. So then I did the social media thing. Their Facebook, Twitter, and Instagram accounts have all been taken down."

"How do you know they were taken down? Maybe they never had any of those accounts. They're not teenagers anymore. Not all of us pre-millennials do that stuff."

"Point taken. But, first of all, for none of them to have any social media presence at all? Highly unlikely. And second, after a bit of kernoodling I found that all of them had posted regularly on their friends' Facebook pages and tweeted, also."

"Until when?"

"Until I called them. That's when they were shut down. I have a feeling someone's got them in their crosshairs and they're scared stiff. They're hiding from me and there's no way to contact them."

"Why don't you write them?"

"What do you mean?"

"As in a letter. As with a pen and paper. Like our ancestors used to do. That you put in the mail with a stamp. Tell them you realize they're afraid of whoever's been threatening them and that they need to tell us the truth."

"The truth will set them free, huh?"

"Make them the same offer Santos and I were going to."

"Things have changed since then, apparently. When you were about to make that offer, you didn't know the women were still being intimidated, as they now seem to be. So the question is, how can they tell the truth without exposing themselves?"

"Offer them witness protection."

"FBI does that, not reporters."

"Then tell them to contact you by writing back. We can get a post office box. Tell them to address their response to some kind of sweepstakes offer, maybe a free trip to Cancun. Cancun Sweepstakes, care of the box number. No one will suspect that."

"How long should we give them?"

"Not sure. A week?" Whitmore, having no idea how long Botford could tolerate the postponement of his extradition, is shooting from the hip, which doesn't make for a very good aim.

"Okay," Duckworthy says. "In the meantime, I'll go through all my Stolz files. Again. Maybe something'll pop up at me. You would've made a good investigative reporter, Ballard. I'll get on that letter right away."

"Just don't mention my name."

Chapter Eighteen

A week later, Whitmore hasn't heard anything from Duckworthy. He has also lost his job at El Chico's. He has been breaking too many dishes of late, the most recent one a ceramic serving platter, *pintado a mano en méxico*. His employer told him he could tell that Whitmore's heart isn't in his work anymore. He only wants employees who are passionate about their work.

Whitmore returns to his room. He is starting to second guess the trust he has placed in Duckworthy. He's tired of waiting and calls her.

"Why haven't you called?" Whitmore asks.

"Because I haven't heard back from the women," she answers.

"Can't you do something?" He is trying not to sound testy. Evidently, he isn'tsuccessful.

"Calm down, big boy. The idea to write them a letter was yours, remember?"

He pulls himself back. Sandy Duckworthy may be his only lifeline left.

"So where do we go from here?"

"Now that you ask, I've been mulling over a backup plan, just in case. A while ago, I did a piece for the *Ledger* on a Sequence regional conference. There was a very accommodating regional director who bought me a beer. Three, in fact, if I remember correctly. Might've been more, but after three, my thinking got a little foggy."

"Is there a point to this?"

"I'm getting there. The thing is, I remember him bragging about how he was able to put the bill on the conference's tab. What I'm getting at is this: It seems to me, between the time you disavowed the Sequence and two days later, when the girls accused you of molesting them, someone had to come up with $40,000 cash, and pronto."

"More than beer money."

"More than beer money. Not too many people have that kind of cash in their wallets or checking accounts, but if your theory is correct that Layton Stolz is behind all this—"

"Then maybe it's in one of the Sequence accounts?"

"That's my thinking, yes. That it's got to be on their books somewhere. And with the way the Stolz machine prides itself on being militantly top down, and on how disciplined they are controlling their finances, you'd think any substantial amount of money like that, someone had to give approval for. Like Stolz himself, maybe."

"Makes sense. But how are you going to find out? You can't just ask him. After all, he is the president."

"Yes, he is. But the BSA isn't. It's a 501(c)(3) nonprofit. They're required to make their tax returns and other significant financial records public."

"But the BSA is a tree with a million branches. Where are you going to start? As my attorney is fond of reminding me, my extradition clock is still ticking."

"I know, so I've tried to narrow it down. Process of elimination. I figure that the local chapters would be hard-pressed to have that much cash hanging around, and that BSA Central would be too smart to keep an expense like that on their own ledgers. So, I'm thinking the regional conferences. There are only eight or ten of those. I can start with them."

"Even so, that could take weeks. Months. And do you know how to examine finances? That takes expertise."

"I don't, but I've got someone who does know. The *Flora Daily Ledger* has a cracker jack CPA. Stash Miyazaki. There ain't a dime you can hide from him. He used to work for the IRS and once had an eight-year-old audited for not reporting his piggybank income."

"You're pulling my leg," Whitmore says.

"Yes, I am. I just made that up. But I've got a pretty good hunch Stash'll drool at helping me get a scoop like this."

"You'd make a good investigative reporter, Sandy," Whitmore says, with a smile. He had almost forgotten what one feels like.

"I know."

With the request for their extradition in abeyance, at least temporarily, Ballard Whitmore and Stavros Santos are at liberty to communicate with each other. As far as they know, the proceedings have been put on hold, but, as Slyke reminded Whitmore, one never knows what diplomatic back channels are in play. He could conceivably be extradited any minute. He should really be paying Slyke for his counsel, rosy or not, but at least Slyke is now being good enough to represent him pro bono. Not that there is much choice. Whitmore had just about run out of money.

It is no secret the Irish are up in arms that Whitmore is being shielded and are exerting diplomatic pressure on the Stolz administration to turn Whitmore over to them. With Phillip Valentine under arrest, Whitmore wonders why he is still at liberty. Government inertia? Maybe Valentine is using him as a bargaining chip to avoid prosecution? Maybe Stolz wants to keep him in his clutches but on a long leash to see where he goes? So many maybes, but one thing is certain: It could all change on a dime. Or, from the Irish end, a euro.

Whitmore has already been tried and convicted in the court of public opinion for the murder of Samantha McCollum and is keeping as low a profile as possible without becoming an actual hermit. He has taken to wearing disguises and changing them regularly to avoid confrontation with those out there who are convinced he is a murderer, others who think he is a rapist, and others who hate him because he betrayed Layton Stolz. In many eyes, the last is the most heinous of his alleged offenses.

Today he wears a hat he's purchased at Jack's Joke Shop, a baseball cap with an attached ponytail hanging out the back. He hasn't shaved for a few days, and with dark sunglasses and a tattered jacket thrown over his ratty T-shirt he could be mistaken as one of the many unwashed denizens of this particular sector of south State Street. He certainly doesn't look anything like the clean-cut BYU grad of his previous life. His own mother wouldn't recognize him, and at this point, she probably wouldn't acknowledge him if she did. Though the lost years in prison have come to an end, the lost years of his family will be forever. Unless he can exonerate himself, in which case there might be a remote possibility of reconciliation. Whitmore squeezes that wishful hope out of his mind. There is still too far to go.

They'd agreed to meet at Denny's, his new hangout. Through a window blurred with frost, Whitmore sees Stavros Santos, who has arrived first, sitting in a window booth. He is wearing the same unostentatious gray suit, enabling him to blend into the woodwork without being noticed. What a private detective would wear, Whitmore thinks. Except in this wormy woodwork no one wears a suit. The diner is too crowded for Whitmore's comfort, but with his new disguise he will at least fit in with the rest of the clientele. Whitmore taps Santos on the shoulder. Santos turns to see who it is and starts to tell Whitmore he doesn't have any spare change and to get lost. It is only when Whitmore smiles that Santos recognizes him behind his subterfuge.

"Jesus, Ballard," Santos says. "What's happened to you?"

"Just being cautious, Stavros. The media hasn't been kind to me, and I'd like to avoid the possibility of getting into any more hot water. Like someone shooting me in the head."

"You're being a little melodramatic I think," Santos says, "if not downright paranoid."

Santos has already been served his coffee. Whitmore is going to order his default Mountain Dew. Instead, he orders coffee, black. Not that he is going to drink any of it. Only to stay in character. Maybe I am being paranoid? he asks himself. I don't care, is his answer.

Whitmore tells Santos about Duckworthy's plan. More of a hope than a plan at this point. The cracker jack accountant, Miyazaki, is already cracking open the BSA's books. He has found them to be immensely complicated and so far hasn't turned up anything promising. But that is better than the response to the letters Duckworthy had written to the three women, which is no response at all. So much for winning a free trip to warm, sunny

163

Cancun. Santos explains that his own lawyer is trying to pull strings to get his extradition request quashed permanently, which sounds similar to what Whitmore's lawyer, Richard Slyke, is doing.

"You'd think they could work together," Santos says. "It would save time and a helluva a lot of money. Those lawyers."

A deafening blast shatters the restaurant window, sending a shower of glass shards over Whitmore. He glances at Santos, who is slumped over the table with a neat red hole where his left eye used to be. One shot, but there is no doubt that Santos is dead. Whitmore dives under the table, blood, brains, and coffee dripping off its edge. Surrounded by panicked cries and screams, he is immobilized by fright until he hears someone shout, "Call the police!" In the pandemonium, and along with other fleeing customers, the more needy of whom help themselves to whatever food they can grab on their way out, Whitmore slips out of the restaurant. Fighting his rushing adrenaline and his inclination to run as fast as he can, he buddies up with a group of vagrants pushing their carts filled with blankets and stuffed black plastic bags, and forces himself to stroll aimlessly with them. He offers to push a cart that a stout, wild-eyed woman, wearing army boots and with sores on her face, is struggling with. The superficial cuts on his own face from the flying glass help him blend in better with his newly-adopted family.

At an intersection with a quiet side street, Whitmore separates himself from the others and, in the bitter cold, wanders the low-income residential neighborhood for an hour, keeping his head down, not walking too fast, until he is convinced no one is following him. Waiting until dusk approaches, he returns to his motel room, entering through the back door. He keeps the lights off and lies in his infested bed for the night, thinking and scratching.

The next morning, Whitmore ventures out to the corner 7-Eleven to get a newspaper. He's made the front page of *The Salt Lake Tribune*. "*Downtown Slaying*" the headline reads.

"*Stavros Santos, a veteran Salt Lake City private detective, was slain in broad daylight yesterday afternoon at the Denny's restaurant on south State Street. A manhunt is underway for the disgraced educator, Ballard Whitmore, who had retained the services of Santos. Whitmore, a registered sex offender currently awaiting extradition to Ireland as a person of interest in the murder of native Utahn Samantha Summerhays McCollum, 'may be presumed to be armed and dangerous,' a Salt Lake City police spokesperson said."*

The *Tribune* showed Whitmore's photo, but it was an outdated one and bore no resemblance to the way he looked yesterday, or would look today. He knows that at some point soon, someone who had been at Denny's would provide the police with a description of an unkempt, pony-tailed white male who had been sitting with Santos. They would be on the lookout. Whitmore shaves his three-day-old beard and then—why not—shaves his entire head, and puts on his one clean, button-down shirt. He packs his belongings into a small backpack, which doesn't take very long, and says good-bye to the bedbugs in Room 201 of the Sunset View Motel. Whitmore doesn't need to read the rest of the story. He ditches his ponytail hat and sunglasses in a dumpster behind the shut-up pawn shop, and at the 7-Eleven ATM he cashes out his checking account. He has no fear of going over the maximum permitted withdrawal. From there he walks two miles to the Greyhound station at 300 South and 600 West. There, he buys a one-way ticket to Fort Collins, Colorado, the closest stop to Flora. From there, he'll find his way. Taking a page out of Stewart Wolfe's playbook, Whitmore pays cash for the bus ticket.

Chapter Nineteen

"Jesus! You scared the crap out of me!" Sandy Duckworthy says. She is standing inside the locked storm door of her house, wrapped only in her bathrobe. Ballard Whitmore is on the outside steps, shivering. The view of Duckworthy's figure, which under the alcove light reveals more than she is aware of, helps him forget how cold he is.

"Sorry," he says. "I couldn't take the chance of using my phone or they might have been able to find me. Are you okay? You seem nervous."

"Why should I be nervous? Some guy who looks like a traveling salesman from the Aryan Nation rings my doorbell in the middle of the night. But lucky me, it's only the guy who the papers say shot his bosom buddy in cold blood. So I ask you, why should I be nervous?"

"If you let me in, I'll be happy to explain. I'd rather not be spotted, if you don't mind."

"Why not? What have I got to lose, except my life? Come on in. And I'd offer you a drink, except you don't drink. But I think I'll have one. And yours too, if you don't mind."

He sits at her kitchen table. She pours an OJ from the fridge for him and a Grey Goose for herself from the freezer, on the rocks. She asks if he's hungry. He hasn't eaten all day, he confesses. She isn't the domestic type, she confesses back, but finds a Tupperware container with the remnants of a rotisserie chicken and side salads from Stop & Shop that she'd been pecking at for the last few days. Whitmore eats with his hands and, in between bites, he tells her the details of Santos's murder at Denny's.

"Except it wasn't a murder," he says. "It was an execution."

"An assassination more like. Why do you suppose?"

"For the same reason they killed Samantha McCollum. Other than the three women who have obviously been threatened and are too scared to talk, only McCollum knew the truth behind their accusations. Whoever killed her wanted to make sure she wouldn't talk."

"But why kill her and not the others?"

"Because she's the only one who didn't take the money. That's why. And when they saw that Santos and I had gotten there before them, they realized they were too late, so then they also had to get rid of the people she talked to. Us."

"How do you know it was *them* who were out to kill you and Santos? How do you know it wasn't Samantha McCollum's family, out for revenge? Maybe they figured if you had escaped extradition, the only justice you'd see would be from their own hands. Those things do happen, you know. Or even Heather Hansen's family, or the other girls'? They all had it in for you, Ballard, especially after McCollum's murder, and then with our pressure tactics to get them to open up, which I guess have backfired royally. But how did they—whoever 'they' are—know you were even in Ireland in the first place? As far as we know, the only people who knew what you and Santos were up to were Valentine's, not Stolz's, and Valentine had every reason to want to keep her alive. She would've been his best bargaining chip by far against Stolz. The last thing he'd want is for her to be killed."

"I know, I know. The only thing I can think of is that somewhere along the line—when we found out there was a fifth girl and her identity, or when we contacted Valentine's people—somehow Stolz's gestapo found out we were getting closer, and started keeping tabs on us. We know someone followed us all the way to McCollum's parents. And then Santos and I led them directly to Samantha. In a way, I'm responsible for her death, and I'm having a hard time getting around that."

"Don't even think that, Ballard. You're just trying to find out the truth."

"Yeah."

"But I need to ask you a question. And forgive me if this sounds harsh but, as you say, we need to get answers and I'm a nosy reporter. If killing Santos had something to do with McCollum's murder, why didn't they try to kill you too?"

"I've been wondering the same thing. And I'm pretty sure it's because they didn't recognize me. I was disguised. They thought I was just some street person bumming for free coffee. Killing a second person, a stranger, would've been collateral damage they didn't need. But now that I've gotten away, they'll be after me."

"Wait a second! Didn't both you and Santos give independent statements to the judge? Didn't you both tell them what Samantha McCollum said to you about the girls? I mean, the cat's already out of the bag."

"If only. But that's not the way the wheels of justice turn when it comes to extradition. We don't have an opportunity to provide that information until there's a hearing. *If* there's a hearing. And you know what my testimony will be worth then? Less than my bank account. First of all, why would anyone believe us? Samantha's dead, and they're convinced we did it. Do you think they're going to believe our story, that minutes before she was murdered she admitted to us for the first time in her life that eleven years ago Layton Stolz tried to extort her? That four girls, one of whom committed suicide, falsely accused me of sexual misconduct? That they should reexamine an open-and-shut case for which they got the conviction the public demanded? That the president of the United States put out hit orders on innocent people?"

"You make a good point."

"I'm at a dead end, Sandy. You've got to find something. I'm a sitting duck. I won't last much longer."

"Believe me, I've been working on it, Ballard. Stash told me he's onto something. I'll call him first thing, okay? You've just got to hang in there for now, okay?"

Sandy goes to the fridge to pour herself another vodka. When she returns, Whitmore is looking at her curiously.

"I imagine you need a place to stay," she says.

Whitmore stops eating and slides the plate away.

"I was hoping I could stay here under the radar, for a while. Maybe on a couch or something."

Duckworthy puts her drink down and places her hand on Whitmore's newly-shaved head, massaging the little imperfections in its roundness, sliding her fingers down to the facial scratches he'd received from the flying glass.

"Do you ever wear a ring in one ear?" she asks.

"Are you kidding? Why?"

"I've got this Mr. Clean fantasy," she says, kissing the top of his head. "I have this thing about bald men. Have I ever mentioned that?"

"Even bald sex offenders?"

"They're the best kind."

His hand is inside her bathrobe, and he stands up to make it easier for her to find his zipper. He hasn't been with a woman since the nightmare started eleven years before. Before his wife left him. Before he spent nine lonely years in prison. He can't wait any longer. He presses his mouth against hers and she presses back. He pins her on her back on the kitchen table. She tears at his jeans and underpants and grasps his penis, pulling it insider her. He unties her robe and squeezes her breasts, hard. Eyes closed and her head back, she supports herself on her elbows, wrapping her legs around Whitmore's waist. Her right hand falls into Whitmore's dinner plate. As he presses into her, she grabs a handful of potato salad and coleslaw and smears it over his face and stuffs it into his mouth. Covering his lips with hers, the two of them tongue the food back and forth from one mouth to the other.

"You like chicken?" she whispers as she licks his face.

"What kind of question is that?" he pants. "Yeah. I suppose."

"Good. Me, too."

Feeling behind her for the remains of a chicken drumstick, she clutches it and slowly slides it into and then out of his mouth, as far as it will go, both of them licking at it, sucking on it. She wraps an arm around his neck as he rides her, his body spasming out of control. His wraps his arms around her back, pulling her toward him. He wants it to go on forever, but it has been such a long time. He shudders as he empties himself into her. He sinks onto her chest, panting, laughing, and crying at the same time.

"House confinement has its rewards," he says, when his breath returns.

"Mmm. My prisoner. Let's go to bed. I won't get any sleep lying on this table. We can have dessert there. But I'm afraid I don't have any bedbugs to keep you company."

In the morning, Sandy dials Stash Miyazaki's number.

"Don't tell him I'm here, okay?" Whitmore says.

"Duh!" she answers. "How much credibility do you think my big exposé will have if anyone finds out you're my boy toy?"

"Your exposé?"

"You mean, you thought I fucked you because I like you?"

"I'm glad you said that with a smile."

"I always smile."

Miyazaki answers the phone. Sandy whispers to Whitmore, "Go have another glass of milk, big boy. I'll take notes."

"Bingo!" she says to Whitmore a half-hour later. "We're almost there. This is what Stash found out. He's got it documented. At the time you were accused of sexual misconduct, there were only eight BSA regional divisions. On the very day before the allegations were made, five-thousand dollars in cash was withdrawn from each of their accounts. On their tax returns, the withdrawals were itemized as 'miscellaneous reimbursements.'"

"Eight times five-thousand is forty-thousand, the exact amount the girls were paid, according to Samantha McCollum."

"Brilliant deduction, Einstein."

"Can't be a coincidence."

"You're on a roll."

"Who made the withdrawals?"

"We don't know that. Yet. But what it means is that all of the regional directors must have known something was going on. And it must have been coordinated from upstairs."

"We need to find out who gave them their marching orders."

"Easier said than done. Most of those regional directors are now highly-placed appointees in the Stolz administration, including the vice president. Getting access to them will be next to impossible, and of course they're all

170

pros at lying their way out of a paper bag."

Whitmore recalls when Vice President Duane Sheely was a troubled high school student in Flora, when Layton Stolz asked him to take Duane under his wing:

"It won't be for long, Ballard. Just until you leave for your mission. In the meantime, I think your example will be a big help to him. Give him a boost."

Of course, Whitmore had agreed, wholeheartedly. It was not just that he had no choice, which he fully understood. He thought of it as training for his mission. Of doing good works. Over the following months, he had tried to befriend Duane, maintaining a positive attitude. Though Duane never protested, Whitmore knew that he had seethed underneath.

"So we're stumped?" he asks Duckworthy.

"Not yet. I was thinking about that time I was at the regional conference in Fort Collins. The director, Darren Witten, is the guy who had some interesting things to say about BSA's finances. He was smooth as silk, but what was interesting was there was one subject that turned him stone-faced."

"What subject was that?"

"You. He would do anything to avoid talking about you. And I mean anything. I think he's one of the few BSA muckamucks who hasn't ended up in the government, so I think I might just renew our acquaintance. After all these years, maybe he'll be ready to share."

Chapter Twenty

"C'mon, Ballard. We're going for a ride."

"I shouldn't be seen in public."

"Don't worry. Where we're going it'll just be a cluster of hunters and gatherers. Not that it does a lot for my ego, but the only use these guys have for newspapers is to start a campfire. And if anyone should ask, you're my cousin Mike from Oshkosh."

"You've got a cousin Mike in Oshkosh?"

"Of course. You don't think I'd lie, do you?"

They drive south on Interstate 25 and turn west onto I-70, leaving the plains and climbing into the Rockies. As they ascend, the snowpack deepens. Even though it is technically spring, in this part of the Rockies the snow dawdles on the mountains until June. After about sixty miles, Duckworthy pulls off the freeway into the small town of Silver Lake and drives a few miles north. She enters the parking lot of the Cougar Canyon Café, finding one of the last spots for her Subaru Impreza in between two souped-up pickup trucks. The bumper sticker on the shiny black one reads, *Don't Tread On Me*. The sticker on the shiny red ones says, *Jesus Is Lord*. That's diversity for you. They both carry gun racks.

Duckworthy and Whitmore have driven all that way for a meeting with Darren Witten. The only former regional Sequence director who has steered clear of public office, Witten has taken the easier road, retiring early on a comfortable pension and living the good life, fly-fishing and playing golf in the bracing mountain air. The first Saturday of every month, he pulls his string bass out of the closet and jams at a local bar with three much older retirees who call him Junior. Witten could be the key to the whole puzzle if they play their cards right. Sandy has brought a hidden recording device to use as evidence, if necessary, which she keeps tucked away where no true gentleman would dare go.

"I thought that's illegal," Whitmore had asked.

"Can go either way. Depends on what judge you ask and what state you're in. But just in case, that's why I brought you along. So that I've got someone who'll say that every word I 'remembered' is accurate, even if we aren't allowed to use the recording."

The café is bustling. The simple chalked blackboard advertises a varied menu as waitresses, Hispanic for the most part, hustle with trays of omelets and enchiladas. Booming, bad music cuts through loud, friendly conversation. Sandy was right. No one pays Whitmore a bit of attention, except for the large black man with cropped graying hair, dressed in jeans and a Milan soccer jersey, waving at them from a corner booth. He stands up, his smile modified by apparent surprise.

"Hello, Sandy. Long time, no see. I thought you said you were coming alone."

"Oh, I decided to bring along someone special."

"Hi," Whitmore says. "I'm Sandy's cousin—"

"Ballard Whitmore," Sandy says.

Whitmore is shocked.

"I thought—"

"Everyone but Darren, Ballard. We trust Darren. Don't we?"

Witten looks at Whitmore and then at Sandy. He appears distressingly conflicted. He shakes his head and reaches for his phone.

"Sandy, I've read the news. Mr. Whitmore here is a fugitive, wanted for—"

"Put the phone away, Darren. I know all about what he's wanted for, but here he is, and I want you to hear his story, his whole story, before you make any phone calls. Because I believe—*I know*—that he's innocent of everything he's ever been accused of."

"Sandy, do you feel safe enough with him being here? I mean..."

"Don't worry. We're safe. Let's all have Cougar Canyon's famous breakfast burrito with pork green chili and catch up on good times, okay?"

The burrito is huge, but even in the time it takes Whitmore to finish it, he has still not totally brought Witten up to the present. With more customers arriving and the tables full, Duckworthy and Witten get refills on their coffee. Whitmore contents himself with another OJ.

They will likely be asked to leave soon, to vacate the table for regulars waiting outside the doorway, whose patience is justifiably wearing thin on a blustery, cold day, so Duckworthy begins to prod Witten with questions about BSA's financial structure. Witten looks back and forth at the two of them sitting side by side opposite him, as if deciding whether, and how much, he can divulge. He sighs.

"As you know," Witten says, "I'm under orders not to talk about our finances to anyone, under any circumstances. But now, what you're telling me, that can't be swept under the rug. Yes, I do remember a request to have my staff withdraw five thousand dollars from our account. It was very out of the ordinary, to say the least. Which is another reason I didn't tell you about it. But the thing is, I never knew what it was for. It was like, just be the good soldier and follow orders. Assume it's for the greater good. Part of the system. You know how the Stolz machine works."

"And that's why you got out?" Whitmore asks. "You got sick of the machine."

"I suppose you could say that. Too much of a good thing is still too much."

Witten smiles at Duckworthy. Whitmore notices the exchange, but says nothing. Duckworthy finds Whitmore's thigh under the table, and gives it a squeeze. Ancient history, the squeeze tells him. Don't fret, you're my boy, now.

"But here's the sixty-four-thousand dollar question, Darren," Sandy says. "Or should I say the forty-thousand dollar question. Who was it that called you to tell you to withdraw those funds? That's the key."

"I really shouldn't say," Witten say.

"Goddamn it!" Whitmore says. He surprises himself. Even after nine years of prison hell, it is the first time in his life he has ever blasphemed. "Sorry. But my life is at stake here. And why? Because I've been set up, over and

174

over again, simply because I wanted to teach music my own way! Music! Sometimes I can't believe what I'm saying, it sounds so ridiculous. But it's true!"

"For you, it was just music," Witten says, "and I don't mean to put you down by saying 'just' music. Hell, you and I, we're both musicians. We're brothers like that, so I know what you're saying. But as far as Layton Stolz is concerned, the least dissension in the ranks can cause a ripple effect. If you're allowed to get away with your own version of the Sequence, what's to prevent others from doing the same and causing everything he had built up to come crashing down? The whole ball of wax. Mind you, I don't personally believe all that would necessarily have happened, but what *I* believe doesn't count. It's what *he* believes. And many others. And it isn't just the money part. It's all about purity. Purity of a program. Purity of a plan. Purity of an ideal. You have to agree, that program inspired literally millions of people."

"Ballard's almost finished with his orange juice and there are folks waiting for the table," Sandy says. "Let's cut to the chase. Which one of the others called you, Darren?"

"All right," Witten says. He surveys the restaurant as if someone might be spying on them. This gives Whitmore little comfort.

"Sheely."

"Duane Sheely?" Whitmore asks. He is stunned. Sheely. Responsible for putting him in prison! What had Whitmore done to him to be repaid like that?

"No way, Darren," Sandy says. "That can't be."

"Why not?" Witten asks. He sounds surprised Duckworthy hasn't taken him at his word. So is Whitmore.

"Because I studied the whole damn BSA organizational chart until my eyes crossed. There were eight regions, each beholden to BSA Central and only to BSA Central. Sheely might be vice president now, but at the time he was only the director of the Midwest region. So maybe he could tell someone in his office to squeeze money from their budget, but he had no authority over any of the other regions. They would've reported him to Stolz if he tried to pull something like that. Uh-uh, Darrin, there's got to be someone else.

Someone higher up the food chain."

Witten squirms. Whitmore has always thought squirming was simply a literary device you read in a book that described a person's unease. But it is really true. The big man sitting opposite him shifts his weight back and forth so much it makes his own booth bench sway.

"All right," Witten says. "You're a reporter, Sandy. I respect that and understand that somehow sooner or later this is all going to get into the open. But may I ask you to keep my name out of it? And I mean entirely. Because"—he looked at Whitmore—"you know what can happen."

"Yes, I can agree to keep you out of it. But only if you give me the name."

Witten looks around him again.

"Duane Sheely was the one who called and told us what we had to do. That's the truth. But the one who authorized the withdrawals was Ann Smith. She and Stolz were the only ones who had that authority. Sheely was their enforcer. But you didn't hear that from me."

"Thank you, Darren. I really appreciate this."

Duckworthy and Whitmore are driving back to Flora on I-70. They're not ready for a celebration yet, but they're ready to talk about what one might be like if everything continues to move in the right direction. A quiet, intimate dinner at a classy French restaurant. A bottle of Sancerre for the lady, a glass of milk for the gentleman. They even laugh about it.

A spring snow squall had started while they were in the restaurant. On the road, flurries are quickly thickening into a white out. Visibility is negligible and the road becomes snow-covered. Duckworthy's windshield wipers are fighting a losing battle against the accumulation of snow and ice. She reduces her speed to thirty. As they descend from the mountains, so too does Whitmore's euphoria of their discovery.

"Sandy, we still don't have an eyewitness, or anyone to say what those withdrawals were used for. They could say it was to pay for flowers or the annual Beethoven party."

"Don't worry, Ballard," Duckworthy says. "A newspaper is not a court of law. A newspaper is a court of public opinion. We state the facts as we know them, and let the story lead readers to draw their own conclusions. When

I lay it all out, the chronology with the financial data Stash unearthed—all legally, mind you—serious questions will be asked. Investigations will be initiated. The full truth will come out and you will be exonerated. I promise you."

Which is the moment the pickup truck behind them rammed the back of Duckworthy's car. They had been descending sharply, accelerating due to the steep grade, and were going around an outside curve when they were hit.

Duckworthy slams on the brakes. It is not the right thing to do. The car spins a slow-motion one-hundred-eighty degrees. They are sliding downwards and backwards towards a sheer drop-off on what had been their right side. As they careen out of control the truck hits them again, this time in the hood. It is the shiny red pickup that they had parked next to at the café. *Jesus Is Lord*. This time the impact flips the Impreza over. Time to start praying.

Whitmore looks at Sandy as they slide upside down and backwards toward the precipice on the snow-packed road. Physically she looks unharmed but her eyes are devoid of expression, as if she has shut herself down, as if she has already given up on life and just wants to spare herself the pain. Her hands aren't even on the steering wheel, and why should they be? Whitmore asked himself. You can't steer an upside down car. He closes his eyes. They had gotten so close to the truth. To each other.

The car caroms off a snowbank once, twice, and again, as if they are inside a pinball game, heading into a massive wall of icy snow that has been plowed at the base of the curve. When they crash into it, the car shudders and groans. Some part of the frame gives way. Like the ball on a roulette wheel, the centripetal force of the curve causes the car to climb the snowbank, flipping it back onto its wheels, still pointed backwards, and bringing it to a thudding stop on the freeway shoulder.

Not until then had they realized the extent of the din they had just endured. Now, the silence is almost as frightening, as if the roaring had become their permanent status quo. So they sit in the silence, too traumatized to speak. They wait for the pickup to come back and finish them off, but there is only the silence.

Sandy shakes her head into consciousness and tries to focus her eyes on Whitmore. She speaks softly.

"Are you alive?" she asks.

"I'm not sure. But if I'm talking, I suppose I am."

"I'll call the police," she says.

"No, don't."

"Why not?"

"Because then they'll find out who I am. It'll be my death warrant as much as the guy who tried to kill us."

"What do we do then?"

"Can you start the car?"

"Are you kidding?"

"We just had one miracle. Let me get out and check the damage."

The snow continues to fall. By the time he has circled the car, he is covered. With his shaved head he looks like Frosty. But he is hopeful. Yes, there are dents and scratches, yes. A rear light is shattered. The luggage rack has been ripped off, and the top of the car is inches lower than it was designed to be. The front bumper is gone but the hood is not nearly as damaged as he had feared. With the car sliding backwards when it was hit in front, it had been spared the brunt of the impact. And the snow on the road and the snowbanks had cushioned what could have been the knockout punch. He gets back in the car.

"Turn the key."

It starts.

"Gotta love those Subarus," Sandy says.

They drive back to Flora, slowly, taking side routes to avoid being noticed by the Highway Patrol, who would be curious why someone in a half-demolished car is out driving in the middle of a raging blizzard.

Darren Whitten calls Duane Sheely with bad news. Whitmore and Duckworthy have escaped. The trucker who Whitten had paid a thousand dollars to ram the Subaru reported that the car, incredibly, was gone when he returned to the scene a half-hour later to confirm the kill.

"I did what you told me to do," the trucker said to Whitten. "I ran them off the road and flipped the damn car. You think for a shitty thousand bucks I'm going to follow them all over hell?"

For allowing them to get away, Sheely berates Whitten even more viciously than Whitten had berated the trucker. Whitten suggests all is not lost. The sense he got from their meal together is that Whitmore and Duckworthy are an item, and that since they were driving together in her car, chances are they were going to her house. He can easily get her address and they can finish the job there.

Sheely doesn't like it. It would be that much harder to make it look like an accident.

"If you're feeling squeamish," Whitten suggests, "why don't you ask Layton?"

"I decide that," Sheely bristles. "And it would serve you to remember his name is no longer Layton. His name is President Stolz. To you and everyone else."

Sheely reports to President Stolz on the unsatisfactory developments, emphasizing it was no fault of his own, and proposes what Whitten had suggested. Engage Whitmore at Duckworthy's house.

"Is there no other option?" Stolz asks. He feels deeply troubled, almost as much by his affection for Whitmore and the young man's friend, the reporter, as by the fact that they are still alive. He recalls the first time he ever spoke to Ballard Whitmore, during that first year of the Sequence in Flora, so long ago. A sweet boy, Ballard, a special boy. Maybe that's why Stolz had lain a hand on the boy's head. It had almost felt like a blessing.

"We can't think of a better one," Sheely says. "We're confident we know how to find him right now. But after tomorrow, who knows?"

"Very well," Stolz says. It is almost as if he is sacrificing a son. "Do what you must, Duane. But, between you and me, it makes me very sad."

Chapter Twenty-One

"Your good buddy, Darren, set us up," Whitmore says.

"We don't know that for sure," Duckworthy answers.

"It had to have been. You assured me a hundred times no one else knew we were meeting him. You saw how he was glancing around at the restaurant? I thought he was worried someone was spying on us. He was just signaling his Born Again goons to run us off the road."

"It could've been someone followed us there."

"For two hours? On those roads? If I learned anything from Stavros, it was how to notice someone following me. I don't think so."

"I don't think so, either."

It had long been dark when they'd arrived back at Duckworthy's house. She'd turned off the headlights a block away and eased the car into the garage so no one could see the damage. The car would stay there for the foreseeable future. They examined themselves for injuries. Miraculously, they had survived even more intact than the car. Some cuts and scratches, bruises, a stiff neck, an arm that couldn't be lifted more than halfway. But they're alive. Nothing that some first aid and a little time won't cure. Well, maybe somewhat more than a little. They take a long, hot bath and go to bed, too exhausted to make love but thankful they will live to see another day.

In the morning, Sandy is being domestic, scrambling some eggs. A return to normalcy, and they're starving, not having eaten since their famous burrito at the café. After breakfast, Sandy will spend the day organizing her compiled notes, which she has backed up on her computer. Her story is almost ready to go to press. And the sooner the better. Only when it's out in the open will they be protected from enemies, seen and unseen. Whitmore steps outside to retrieve the *Fort Collins Coloradoan* on the front doorstep.

"Forget the eggs, Sandy," he says. "We have to get out of here. Now."

"Why?" she asks.

He shows her the front page. There's a closeup photo of Whitmore's face. Fortunately, it's his mugshot from when he was arrested long ago for the sexual misconduct charges. Not surprisingly, he looks somber in the photo, more muscular than he is now, ten years more youthful, and of course there's a headful of hair. The photo looks very little like his current appearance.

The *Coloradoan* is carrying an AP wire story of a massive national manhunt for Ballard Whitmore, primary suspect in the slayings of Samantha McCollum and Stavros Santos. He should be considered armed and definitely dangerous. An anonymous tip—no doubt Witten's doing—has narrowed the manhunt to Colorado. The captain of Colorado Highway Patrol assured the public, "It's only a matter of time." The State Department, with President Stolz's explicit blessing, has approved his extradition to Ireland. Once the winner is determined in the tug-of-war between Ireland and the US for who will be first to have the pleasure to try Whitmore for murder, he will certainly be facing either life imprisonment or execution, depending on the jurisdiction.

They don't dare drive the Subaru. In its condition it would raise too many eyebrows even if it started, which is by no means a certainty. Sandy calls Uber, and a driver arrives in five minutes. They jump in with nothing other than her laptop. As they turn the corner at the end of her street, a silver Acura is driving toward them. Whitmore hides his face behind his copy of the *Coloradoan* so that the Acura driver will only be able to see Whitmore's frontpage mugshot as he passes by. Little does he know that the real thing is behind it, Whitmore thinks. On the other hand, Whitmore has never seen the Acura driver's face, either, and hopes he never will.

Duckworthy has the Uber driver drop them off a block from the Flora train station, near a down-in-the-dumps part of town. She doesn't give the driver a specific destination because she doesn't want him to be able to tell the police where they're going in case they trace them this far. And if the police do, the driver would probably tell them his passengers were going somewhere by train, because as they're driving, she improvises a story with Whitmore—just loud enough for the driver to overhear—about an Amtrak train they're going to connect to in Denver.

But they don't go into the train station. Instead, in the chill of the morning, under brooding clouds, they slip along ice-covered, broken-up sidewalks, past boarded-up strip malls, and arrive at the Pillow Talk Motel.

"Why did you pick this dump?" Whitmore asks.

"They take cash," Duckworthy replies. "No credit card tracing. No questions asked. They charge by the hour."

"How do you know all this?" Whitmore asks.

"You ask too many questions."

"Just curious. Really, how do you know this stuff?"

"Okay, I'm an investigative journalist, all right? It's my job to know 'stuff'," Duckworthy says with a smile, and pats him on the cheek. At the front desk, she pays Jinks, an unkempt man of indeterminate age and ethnic ancestry, forty-nine dollars for the twenty-four hour special, which otherwise would have been six dollars per hour. Duckworthy signs them in as Eleanor and Franklin Roosevelt. Jinks doesn't bat an eyelash. Room 316, third floor, down the hallway. Duckworthy gives Jinks a five-dollar tip.

Fortunately, their room has electricity, though little more. It is even shabbier than the Sunset View, and Whitmore would open the window to let out the stink of stale cigarettes, beer, body odor, and worse, if the windows weren't screwed shut. Instead, Whitmore stands lookout, peering out the window while hiding himself with the curtain in front of him. All day, Duckworthy writes her story and from time to time checks the internet for any updates on the manhunt.

"Ballard," Duckworthy says. "I just read that Layton Stolz is making a major announcement from the Oval Office at five o'clock."

"What's it about?"

"No one knows, but I'm sure it will be interesting."

At five o'clock they turn on the television. It's probably the last tube television set in the world. The color is grainy. But it works.

"My fellow Americans, it is my privilege to make an important announcement," President Stolz begins. He appears at ease, looking directly into the camera, directly at his flock, his hands folded on his desk. It is obvious he isn't reading off a monitor. It is abundantly clear he is speaking from the heart.

"We honor America in so many ways," he says. "On the Fourth of July, we raise our flag with pride to celebrate our independence from tyranny. In schools across the country, our children recite the Pledge of Allegiance. 'With liberty and justice for all,' the mission of our democracy. In perhaps the most public way, we honor America before every sporting event with the singing of our beloved national anthem. Our *Star Spangled Banner*. This has been, and always will be our sacred tradition. However, when the excitement of the game is over, when we return to our homes with our families, we often leave those feelings of national pride at the ballpark, at the arena, at courtside. As we go about our daily business, we sometimes place that sense of national unity in abeyance until the next game, which may be days, weeks, or even months later.

"I've often asked myself, is there something we can hold onto, together, to keep that bond strong and firm? Even strengthen it? The answer, my fellow Americans, came to me last night in a dream. Yes, a dream. And in the dream, I received a message from none other than Ludwig van Beethoven, himself. The same Beethoven whose inspiring music has, for almost the past two decades, given us so much to be thankful for: improving our schools, lowering our crime rate, giving our young people not only glorious music but also the gifts of discipline, engagement, teamwork, cooperation. Giving them hope for a bright future. To work hard, to strive for something so great, *and to achieve it*, is a gift to be reckoned with.

"Actually, what the Master said to me was not so much a message as an invitation. In the dream, Beethoven said to me, 'Please use my music to bring glory unto your nation, to spread the message of brotherhood.' I asked, how shall I? How can I, your humble servant, do that? And Beethoven said, 'You will know. You will know.' And then the dream faded, as all dreams do, sooner or later.

"But when I awoke, I knew exactly what Beethoven wanted me to do! Because, you see, today, March 26, is no random date. Because it was on this day, March 26, in 1827, when Beethoven closed his eyes on the world for the last time. His last mortal act was to raise his fist to the heavens, and at the very moment he fell back onto his bed, dead, there was such a terrible clap of thunder over Vienna that it shocked the entire city. This is true. Historians have confirmed this."

Stolz's face fills the screen, and transforms itself from the intensity of his vision to something much more benign, almost fatherly, with a hint of a smile.

"It is fitting that a few short days from now will be the start of another season of our national pastime, baseball. A truly American game, *the* American game, which, coincidentally, was invented only a few short years after Beethoven's death. Accordingly, I have issued an executive order that from this day forward, any event which we begin with the singing of the *Star Spangled Banner* we will end with the singing of the inspirational *Ode to Joy* from Beethoven's Ninth Symphony. For this purpose, I have replaced Friedrich Schiller's German lyrics, which Beethoven used, with my own, to reflect our devotion to our country and our faith in our leaders. I don't have a particularly good singing voice, but it goes something like this."

President Stolz clears his throat and takes a deep breath.

"Patriots join thy hands together,
Striving for our liberty.
Triumph over foes abroad
To keep our homeland safe and free.

Ever forward!
Never complacent!
Faith in our leaders vigilant.
Shed our blood for truth and glory,
Trusting in our government.

"My fellow Americans, our strength is in our unity. *E pluribus unum*. Out of many, one. It is our national motto. So, what greater, more powerful, more *beautiful* demonstration of *E pluribus unum* can there be than to see and hear every citizen lift their voices together in the singing of our national anthem and of Beethoven's hymn to brotherhood?

"Which is why, today, I am signing two executive orders. The first is to make this hallowed day of March 26, the new national holiday of Beethoven Day. The second makes the singing of the *Star Spangled Banner* and the *Ode to Joy* a legal requirement of every American at all public events.

"Of course, we live in a democracy with inalienable rights. Citizens are free to choose. However, to encourage everyone to join together in celebrating our nationhood, I hereby establish a Bureau of Citizen Marshals to engage in private, benevolent persuasion with those few who exercise their right not to participate. I expect that will bring everyone into the fold in a positive manner. However, if there are any remaining, disengaged outliers, we may need to consider further, more assertive methods."

President Stolz's face darkens. He pauses, as if there is something he has planned to add but is reconsidering. His jaw tightens and his eyes seem to roll back into his head. He seems an entirely different human being. The cloud dissipates as suddenly as it had arrived. His eyes refocus, his countenance relaxes, and his benign smile returns.

"But let's see what happens. Thank you all, goodnight, and may God bless America."

Ann Smith is watching from behind the cameras. For the first time in her memory, there are tears in her eyes. Her hands are on her cheeks as the world falls apart around her. "What has happened to you, Mr. Stolz?" she whispers to herself. "You've gone too far."

"You're questioning the wisdom of Layton Stolz?" Duane Sheely asks.

"I wasn't talking to you."

"But I'm talking to *you*. You need to make a decision, Ann. Either you're on board or not."

"And you've gone too far, Duane," Ann Smith replies. "In more ways than one."

"He's insane." Whitmore says, turning away from the television.

"Astute observation, Professor Ballard," Sandy says. "Call out for some pizza. I'm starving, and I've got to finish writing this before it's too late. For everyone."

When Whitmore goes to sleep sometime after midnight, Duckworthy is still at the computer and has taken advantage of the room's single luxury item, a Mr. Coffee coffeemaker. Whitmore doesn't even interrupt her to say goodnight. The next morning, the sky is still dark, the pot is empty—he doesn't know how many times it had been filled—and her story is finished. She has chronicled the entire saga, starting from the Stolz machine's first effort to silence Ballard Whitmore almost thirteen years before with its whispering campaign of letters to the editors of the Salt Lake City newspapers, letters that were subtly critical of Whitmore's volunteer efforts; and ending with the attempt on their lives two days earlier. Before she sends it off to the *Daily Ledger,* as a professional she feels it is her journalistic obligation to contact everyone she is naming in her story to invite their response and include their side of it, should they so desire. Otherwise, it could easily be labeled commentary or, far worse, seditious propaganda. Ordinary, innocent citizens were starting to be hauled away in increasing numbers under that charge. Duckworthy's list includes President Layton Stolz, Vice President Duane Sheely, Chief of Staff Ann Smith, former Secretary of State Phillip Valentine, his aide Stewart Wolfe, the three women who had accused Whitmore of sexual misconduct—Kimberlea Heath Shay, Lexi Briscoe Adamson, Joy Sparks Madison—and Ballard Whitmore himself. Most of them, either directly or through their spokespeople, refuse to accept her call. Of the few who talk to her, all but one threaten legal action and hang up, which Duckworthy considers a sign that her story has hit the mark. The one person who agrees to be quoted is Ballard Whitmore: "I know that when the whole truth comes out the world will know I'm innocent. This is the first step." Duckworthy's last call goes to someone special. She regrets he doesn't answer the phone, so she leaves a message on his answering machine:

CHAPTER TWENTY-ONE

"Hello, Darren! This is your old drinking buddy, Sandy Duckworthy…"

There is a distant siren. Police. It comes closer.

"I think they've found us," Whitmore says. "We've got to get out of here."

Duckworthy presses Send on her email. The story will go public, rough edges and all, with or without her. She grabs her computer and her purse. Whitmore looks out the window. Police cars—three, four, five of them—pulling up to the Pillow Talk, sirens shrieking, lights flashing. A SWAT team arrives. Armed officers streaming out of the cars, guns in hand. One of them looks up and sees him. He's been spotted. They surround the motel. Whitmore hears the motel's doors slamming. Footsteps speeding up the stairway. There's no way out.

"This is it," he says to Sandy Duckworth. "They're going to kill me. You stay here. I'm going down there."

"Hold on, Ballard. This might just be the best thing that could have happened to you."

"Are you nuts? There's an army out there!"

Sandy gets on her cellphone and calls the front desk.

"Jinks, this is Eleanor Roosevelt. Put a cop on the line. Any cop."

It doesn't take long.

"Officer, this is Sandy Duckworthy, senior correspondent with the *Flora Daily Ledger*. I am here with Ballard Whitmore. We are in Room 316. We are unarmed. We are going to open our door and lie face down on the ground with our hands above our heads. Please don't shoot us. We are giving ourselves up."

Whitmore can't believe what Sandy has just done.

"You just signed my death warrant, Sandy."

"You think so? I think I just saved your life, Ballard. The cops are our protection. We stay alive till tomorrow, there's no way Layton Stolz can get to us."

Chapter Twenty-Two

Emblazoned on the front page of the *Flora Daily Ledger*, in the biggest font that would fit, is the headline: *President Implicated In Murder, Extortion.* Occupying seven entire pages of the paper's eight-page main section, Sandy Duckworthy's exposé makes no explicit accusations. It simply lays out the chronology and the facts. Most damning are the financial statements indicating the systematic withdrawal of forty-thousand dollars from eight separate regional BSA accounts at exactly the same on the same day that four teenage girls were coerced into committing perjury, the consequence of which sent Ballard Whitmore to prison for nine years. According to a reliable confidential source, the withdrawal was ordered by Vice President Duane Sheely and authorized by White House Chief of Staff Ann Smith, who at the time were highly-placed BSA administrators. Dissecting the autocratic internal structure of the BSA organization, Duckworthy asks the inevitable questions that will soon be on everyone's lips: What did President Layton Stolz know and when did he know it?

And then the coverups, which included the cold-blooded slayings of Samantha McCollum—the so-called "fifth girl"—and of private investigator Stavros Santos, and the attempted murder of Ballard Whitmore and the reporter herself. There are still enough dots that will need to be connected and enough questions to be asked that endless congressional investigations and the appointment of a special prosecutor are a fait accompli. Sandy Duckworthy has caused a national uproar. The story spreads like a tsunami, engulfing the Beltway and rocking it to its political foundations.

President Layton Stolz, sitting as his desk in the Oval Office, chews thoughtfully on a bologna sandwich. The simple things. Where have they all gone?

"First we disavow," Duane Sheely says, standing opposite him. "Totally disavow. I'll personally call every BSA chapter and have them slam a Beethoven in front of every newsroom, every radio station, every television station that dares to spread this bullshit."

"No need for language like that, Duane."

"We'll do it just like we did with Valentine and with Harrington. We have all the support we need. More than the support we need. By the end of the week, there won't be one media outlet that'll dare to say a word against your administration."

"It could work," Stolz says. "But what about the young lady? The reporter. She seems to be a difficult one to silence."

"Let me take care of her," Sheely says. "She'll regret—"

"Stop!" Ann Smith says. She is standing next to Sheely. "Just stop."

"But why, Ann?" Stolz says. "Do you have a problem with Duane's plan? You don't think it will work?"

"Layton," she says. "Listen to me. It doesn't matter whether it works or not, whatever 'works' means. This country is turning into a police state, stifling speech, killing off political enemies."

"How dare you!" Sheely says.

"Go ahead and deny it, Duane," Ann Smith says. "It was your idea to threaten those girls into lying. It was you who ordered the McCollum woman killed, and then the detective. It was you and Witten who tried to have Whitmore and the reporter killed. When is it going to stop, Duane? Layton, make it stop. It has to stop."

"But, Ann."

"Layton, is this the world you think Beethoven would have wanted?"

Stolz was about to take the last bite of his sandwich, but he holds it there in front of his mouth. There's so little left, he thinks. Of anything. How is life like a bologna sandwich? That thought provides him with some quiet amusement. Oh, well. Finishing it can wait. He places it on a plate.

"Thank you, Duane. I think I know what I have to do, but I need to have a private word with Ann. Please leave us. I'll let you know what I decide. Thank you."

Sheely begins to protest. Stolz holds up a hand.

"It's okay, Duane. You know I value your thoughts."

Ann Smith and Layton Stolz are alone.

"Ann, something just occurred to me. Can you believe that after all these years I've never asked you about your past? It seems I really don't know a thing about you. Anything at all. Before I decide on this matter, I'd like to know something about you. Who you are."

Ann Smith appears to consider a response. She hesitates.

"There's nothing much to know. Nothing at all, really."

They look into each other's eyes for a few seconds, after which they both become uncomfortable.

"All right, Ann. I have appreciated your advice. All your help. Thank you."

"Is that all?"

"Yes. That's everything. Thank you."

After she leaves, Stolz is alone. Duane and Ann. Ann and Duane. Which one of you is the Great Dane and which is the poodle? he wonders. He finishes his sandwich, carefully wipes the crumbs off his desk and deposits them into the trash can. He then removes a sheet of presidential stationery from his drawer and, after considering the best words, writes a letter.

Chapter Twenty-Three

A week after Duckworthy's exposé in the *Flora Daily Ledger*, there is a quiet meeting in the living room of the Utah governor's mansion on South Temple. It is discreet, away from the glare of public scrutiny, which would have been unavoidable at his offices at the state capitol building. There are ten people present: three young women with their attorneys, Ballard Whitmore with his, the governor, and his chief legal counsel. Members of the media were not invited.

Sandy Duckworthy had convincingly established that the four women—including the deceased Heather Hansen—who accused Whitmore of sexual misconduct had been coerced. But for Duckworthy, this by no means exonerated them. They had committed perjury for money, and it would be up to the halls of justice, not Sandy Duckworthy, to sort out their tangled legal web. Forced out of their self-imposed anonymity, the three women hired lawyers to defend their actions. Over the past week, Ballard Whitmore's lawyer, Richard Slyke, hammered out a deal with the other attorneys. Hence, the meeting at the governor's mansion.

Whitmore would agree not to pursue any civil action against the women or hold them responsible for his incarceration. The governor would issue Whitmore a full, public pardon, expunging from the record the verdict against him and his designation as a sex offender. And in consideration of the years of imprisonment he had endured, and the loss of his livelihood and family, the state would award him nine-hundred-thousand dollars, one-hundred-thousand dollars for each year of incarceration. A pittance, everything considered, but at least it was an acknowledgement.

191

The state would also agree not to pursue criminal action against the three women for their false testimony against Whitmore. However, Whitmore insisted, with the state agreeing, that the women acknowledge in a signed statement to the effect that, external pressures imposed upon them notwithstanding, their actions, first by lying and then by concealing the truth for years, cast an unfair cloud of doubt over honest testimony of other women whose claims of sexual harassment were legitimate.

Once all the parties signaled their agreement, there would be a straightforward public statement by the governor and life would go on.

"We have a deal then?" the governor asks.

Everyone present nods. The lawyers shake hands.

"Good," the governor says. "We'll have the attorneys pass around the papers for your signatures. This is easy for me to say, but I'm glad we can put this behind us."

If any doubt existed as to the legitimacy of Duckworthy's investigative reporting, they were laid to rest the same day her exposé appeared in print, when President Layton Stolz blasted a hole in his chest with his father's shotgun, obliterating his heart. Yes, he had left a note. No, it would not be made available to the public. The next day, as a stunned nation mourned, Vice President Duane Sheely and Chief of Staff Ann Smith surrendered to the FBI. With the chain of command in the White House in a shambles, the speaker of the House of Representatives, Sheffield Harrington, the victim of Sheely's first Beethoven slam, was appointed president as dictated by the Constitution. Darren Witten, the final co-conspirator, was arrested. Seeking plea deals, Sheely identified the professional underworld hitmen he had hired to kill McCollum and Santos, and Witten IDed the trucker he'd hired to run Whitmore and Duckworthy off the road. Ann Smith suffered a mental collapse. She was hospitalized, under sedation, and unable to be interviewed for the foreseeable future.

Whitmore sips the champagne, the first alcohol of his life. How can anyone like the taste of that? he thinks. He finishes it out of politeness and gingerly places the champagne flute next to the soap dish. He lies back in the tub. The water's heat has dissipated along with his euphoria, but at least this will be his last Motel 6.

"Cat got your tongue?" Sandy asks, facing him.

"Just thinking."

"About what you're going to do with all that money, big guy?" Sandy asks. She digs her toes into his thighs.

"I've got a lot to thank you for. Maybe I ought to buy you a new car."

"How about a tank?"

"Thinking of letting my hair grow back."

"Don't you dare! I meant it when I said I liked baldies."

"Actually, I was thinking of getting back into music. Playing the violin again."

"Great idea."

"And then maybe trying to see my kids. Now that they know their dad isn't a pathological sex pervert."

They let a long silence pass.

"Sorry," he says. "We should be celebrating."

"Damn right," Sandy says. "I've been meaning to tell you. I found out the contents of Stolz's suicide note."

"How did you manage that?"

"Friends in high places. All of a sudden I seem to have a lot of them."

"What did it say?"

"Pretty cryptic stuff. First off, he wrote it to his mother, who's been dead for years. It said, 'I tried my best.'"

"I'm sure in his own disturbed mind he believed it was true. Nothing cryptic about that."

"Maybe not. But it's how he signed it: *Coriolanus.*"

"What did you say?"

"*Coriolanus.*"

Whitmore shoots up in the tub like a Polaris missile. Unaccustomed to alcohol in his bloodstream and with a slippery tub floor, he loses his balance, landing on top of Duckworthy.

"That's more like it, handsome," she says.

"Sandy, I killed him! I killed Layton Stolz!"

"I think you had too much champagne for a first go-round, honey pie."

"You don't understand. I've got to confess something to you."

"Don't tell me you're a priest?"

"Not that easy. This is too weird." Whitmore replies. "Would you mind a little music history lesson?"

"It better be good."

"You can't imagine. You see, Beethoven composed hundreds of sonatas, trios, quartets, songs, masses. Everything. And they're all the work of a genius. But what is he most known for? What is Beethoven most known for?"

"He was deaf."

"Yes, but what about his music?"

"Symphonies?"

"Right. His orchestra music. His overtures. His concertos. His symphonies. That's where his superiority over anyone else, ever, shone the most. Head and shoulders. And do you know what's amazing?"

"You."

"Thank you, but that's not what I mean. Every one of his orchestral pieces ends in triumph. In a major key. With power. With joy. With an exclamation mark of victory. Every single one. That's what moved Layton Stolz to the depths of his soul."

"Is this going somewhere?"

"Stay with me. There was one exception. Only one. And that one is the *Coriolan Overture*, which ends in C minor, fading away, tragically, in defeat. The only one. It's kind of the mirror image of the *Egmont*. Think about that."

"End of story?"

"Beginning of story, Sandy. Gaius Marcius Coriolanus was a Roman general, honored for his valor on the battlefield. But the Roman senate turned its back on him, sending him into exile. He gathered the forces of Rome's enemies, the Volsci, and laid siege to Rome. No emissaries, no ambassadors, no priests, with all their negotiating and all their entreaties, could convince Coriolanus to spare Rome, because Coriolanus was bent upon revenge."

"And did he get it? His revenge?"

"He didn't. After all else had failed, who showed up but his mother, Veturia. And it was only her pleas, the pleas of a mother, that touched him, and he withdrew his army. So Rome survived, but Coriolanus, heartbroken and now a traitor to both sides, did not. In the end, Coriolanus had no alternative but to kill himself."

"I'm starting to get this."

"Beethoven paid homage to Coriolanus's heroism in his music. The restless intensity of C minor depicts the general's grim resolve and divided loyalty. The tender second theme, in the relative major key of E-flat, that's the mother. A mother who loves her son."

"As another great Roman said, the die had been cast."

"Who said that?"

"Julius Caesar," Duckworthy says. "So they say. And that's all very interesting, Ballard, but what does that have to do with you?"

"Years ago, when I first got pushback for straying from the Sequence, I wrote a one-word letter to Layton Stolz. The one word, with a question mark, was *Coriolan*."

"What?" This time, it was Duckworthy who sat straight up. "Ballard, were you threatening Stolz for trying to shut you up? That could change everything! That could put you back in the hot seat!"

"No, Sandy! That's not it at all. That's what's crazy. The *Coriolan Overture* was the piece I happened to be working on with my orchestra at that moment. Because it's so different from everything else Beethoven wrote, I thought Stolz would be interested to add it to the Sequence. I was trying to help him. If only he'd bothered to ask me. I loved the man."

"And so you're telling me now you think your letter might have inadvertently influenced Stolz to kill himself?"

"Until now, I had no idea. I never knew if he ever even received it. But now…"

"You think you were the one who cast the die?"

"It's possible. Stolz thinking of himself as Coriolan. The misunderstood warrior. His mother. Who knows?"

Duckworthy helped herself to more champagne, drinking from the bottle. She looks at Whitmore for a long time.

"So why did you work on the *Coriolan Overture* with your orchestra, anyway?" she asks. "It's a dark message. Were you trying to make some kind of profound point?"

"You know why, Sandy? Because it isn't played very often and it's a beautiful piece of music. Aren't those reasons enough?"

"Good enough for me," Duckworthy says. "Now, how about you and I make some beautiful music together."

Acknowledgements

The Beethoven Sequence started out many years ago as a short-story flight of fancy, based on the musing of what might happen if one of the world's eminently popular violin methods, which for decades has had an almost cult-like following, were to go absolutely over the top. Only in the past year or so did the story come into focus as a full-length thriller with profound political implications.

Guiding me along the route were three people, Josh Getzler, Danielle Taylor, and Jaylyn Olivo. Josh, my agent at HG Literary, provided perspicacious insights into character development and plot expansion. Danielle, a lawyer in Lakeway, Texas, arrived out of the blue on my cyber doorstep to help me navigate the intricacies of international extradition law. (I hope I got it right.) Jaylyn, a friend from Tanglewood Music Festival days and a proofreader nonpareil, corrected several hundred errors I had somehow overlooked.

It goes without saying, thank you to my publisher and editors, Verena Rose and Shawn Reilly Simmons at Dames of Detection/Level Best Books, for your enthusiastic embrace of this project.

About the Author

Gerald Elias leads a double life as a world class musician and critically acclaimed author.

His award-winning Daniel Jacobus mystery series takes place in the dark corners of the classical music world. *Devil's Trill*, his debut novel, was a Barnes & Noble *Discover: Great New Writers* selection. Elias's prize-winning essay, *War & Peace. And Music*, excerpted from his memoir, *Symphonies & Scorpions*, was the subject of his TEDxSaltLakeCity2019 presentation. Many of his short stories and essays have appeared in prestigious journals ranging from *Ellery Queen Mystery Magazine* to *The Strad*.

A former violinist with the Boston Symphony and associate concertmaster of the Utah Symphony, Elias has performed on five continents and has been music director of Salt Lake City's popular Vivaldi by Candlelight chamber orchestra series since 2004. He divides his time between Salt Lake City and West Stockbridge, Massachusetts, maintaining a vibrant concert career while continuing to expand his literary horizons.

Also by Gerald Elias

The Daniel Jacobus mystery series
Devil's Trill
Devil's Trill audio book
Danse Macabre
Danse Macabre audio book
Death and the Maiden
Death and Transfiguration
Playing with Fire
Spring Break

Short mysteries
"...an eclectic anthology of 28 short mysteries to chill the warmest heart"

Nonfiction
Symphonies & Scorpions

Children's
Maestro, the Potbellied Pig
Maestro, the Potbellied Pig audio book
Maestro, el cerdito barrigón (Spanish translation)
Maestro, el cerdito barrigón audio book

Editor
Getting Through: Tales of Corona and Community

Periodical Publications
Fiction:
Ellery Queen Mystery Magazine
Sherlock Holmes Mystery Magazine
Level Best crime fiction anthologies: *Rogue Wave, Windward, Landfall, Noir*

at the Salad Bar
Kwik Krimes
Berkshire Magazine

Nonfiction:
Boston Symphony program books
Opera Magazine
Berkshire Magazine
Stringendo Magazine (Australia)
Reichel Arts Review
The Strad magazine

CPSIA information can be obtained
at www.ICGtesting.com
Printed in the USA
FSHW011722151020
74870FS